THE SHAMED LITTLE MATCH GIRL

Victorian Romance

FAYE GODWIN

Tica House Publishing

Copyright © 2021 by Faye Godwin

All rights reserved.

No part of this book may be reproduced in any form or by any electronic or mechanical means, including information storage and retrieval systems, without written permission from the author, except for the use of brief quotations in a book review.

PERSONAL WORD FROM THE AUTHOR

Dearest Readers,

I'm so delighted that you have chosen one of my books to read. I am proud to be a part of the team of writers at Tica House Publishing. Our goal is to inspire, entertain, and give you many hours of reading pleasure. Your kind words and loving readership are deeply appreciated.

I would like to personally invite you to sign up for updates and to become part of our **Exclusive Reader Club**—it's completely Free to Join! I'd love to welcome you!

Much love,

Faye Godwin

FAYE GODWIN

CLICK HERE to Join our Reader's Club and to Receive Tica House Updates!

https://victorian.subscribemenow.com/

CONTENTS

| Personal Word From The Author | 1 |

PART I
Chapter 1	7
Chapter 2	21
Chapter 3	37
Chapter 4	51

PART II
Chapter 5	59
Chapter 6	67
Chapter 7	78
Chapter 8	91
Chapter 9	100
Chapter 10	116

PART III
| Chapter 11 | 127 |
| Chapter 12 | 139 |

PART IV
| Chapter 13 | 155 |
| Chapter 14 | 169 |

Continue Reading...	172
Thanks For Reading	175
More Faye Godwin Victorian Romances!	177
About the Author	179

PART I

CHAPTER 1

Dinah Shaw hurried up the rickety stairs of the tenement building, her heart pounding with excitement despite the icy drafts that found their way through the holes in the thin, shaky walls. Her right hand was firmly clutched around the small, skinny arm of her five-year-old brother; in her left, she carried something she considered to be a great treasure. It crinkled and rustled promisingly in her hand. Despite the hunger gnawing at the pit of her stomach, Dinah gave a little giggle of happy anticipation.

"Slow down, Di," complained her brother's little voice by her side. "I can't keep up."

"Oh, sorry, Ollie." Dinah slowed a little, tugging at Ollie to bring him beside her. "I just can't believe that I've found a whole entire newspaper. And it's not even wet. It's perfect."

"Mama will take it if she sees you with it," said Ollie.

Dinah looked down into his wide, worried eyes. They were softest brown and looked enormous in his pinched face. "It's a good thing Mama isn't here then," she said, trying to keep her tone as light as she could. "By the time she gets back, I'll be done with it. We'll stuff it into that gap in the wall and she won't even notice."

Ollie's face brightened. "The gap right above your side of the pallet?"

"That's right," said Dinah, wincing at the memory of every cold night spent under that howling draft.

"Oh, good," said Ollie. "Let's go put it in the gap right away."

"Not yet," laughed Dinah. "Newspapers are for reading, Ollie."

"Mama says there's no reason to learn to read," said Ollie. "She says you're a fool for trying it, and that it's no use."

Dinah felt a familiar hurt blaze across her heart. She was fairly certain that Mama hated reading simply because she had never learned herself, and for some reason that Dinah would never understand, the written word frightened her. But she couldn't say that to Ollie. She forced a smile instead. "Maybe I am a bit silly, then," she said, "but we've got to do something to keep busy while Mama's out, don't we? Besides, you can play with the boys while I'm busy."

"Yes." Ollie's face brightened. "Bobby found some nails in the street last week. We're using them as soldiers."

They had reached the top floor of the tenement building now, where the rooms were the smallest of them all, and the wind blew the coldest through the windows with the remnants of their shattered panes jutting out against the wooden boards like teeth made of glass. The doors here were little better; at least Mama had a door, even though it hung drunkenly off one hinge and was missing half a plank from the top. The Morris family next door didn't have a door at all. A tattered curtain stirred in the drafts from outside, barely maintaining what little dignity Aggie, Silas, and their children had left.

Aggie was a broken-down mother of five who always seemed to be on the brink of another bout of the flu, but she had one wonderful amazement that drew Dinah like a moth to a flame: She could read.

"Aggie?" Dinah pitched her voice in the middle of the spectrum between groveling and pleading. "It's me and Ollie. Can we come in?"

There was a beat of silence before Aggie's resigned voice came through the curtain toward them. "I have better things to do than look after some p... some person's children," she grumbled.

"I'll take the little boys back to our tenement in a while," Dinah pleaded. "To give you a little break."

It worked; it always worked with Aggie. "All right, then," she growled. "Come inside."

Dinah pushed aside the grubby curtain. Like her own, the Morris tenement was only two rooms: this one, where three sleeping pallets were pushed up against one corner, and a feeble fire flickered in a cracked stove in the other; and, through another curtain near the back, a tiny, filthy lavatory. Aggie occupied the only chair, stationed near the stove. Something that smelled like potato skins was bubbling in a pot on the stove. The pot was missing one handle. At Aggie's feet, a trio of little boys were engaged in lining up their makeshift toys: rusty nails, little pebbles, half a button.

Dinah felt a familiar, swift pang of disappointment. She smiled at Aggie as Ollie ran over to his little friends. "Is Benjamin out?" she asked.

"He and Pearl are both working," said Aggie. She gave Dinah a glare out of watery eyes that might once have been hazel, but now looked a washed-out yellow, so bloodshot were they. "As you should be, too, girl. You must be twelve or thirteen years old now. Why, I'm surprised old Scully hasn't forced your mother to send you off to the factories yet. Your wages would help with the rent."

"I'm twelve," said Dinah, shuddering a little at the mention of their slimy-haired, twitchy-eyed landlord. "I want to work, but Mama says I have to look after Ollie."

"Humph," snorted Aggie. "Your mother would be better off caring for the child herself instead of..." She stopped, and something softened around the corners of her eyes. "Never mind," she said. "You're here now."

Dinah hated the ugly suspicion that was starting to rise in her stomach each time an adult carefully skirted around her mother's occupation. Mama had always told them that she sold flowers on the street corners, an idea that Ollie still believed wholeheartedly. Dinah wasn't so sure anymore. Other flower-sellers seemed able to come home at night, unlike Mama.

Her fists tightened at the thought, and she felt the paper crinkle in her hands. She'd almost forgotten about it. Lowering her eyes, she said softly, "Aggie, will you help me to read? Please?"

Aggie seemed regretful that she'd mentioned Mama at all. She gave in more easily than normal, letting out a gusty sigh. "Very well," she said. "Bring it here."

Dinah felt a rare bubble of delight rise in her belly. "Oh, thank you, Aggie," she said.

"Just a few words," Aggie added sternly. "I don't have all day. And then you'll take the little ones to your tenement." She softened again. "I've got a bit of fish for you if you want it."

Dinah was careful to temper her response, even though the prospect of real food for supper made her heart race. "That would be very nice, please."

"Very well," sniffed Aggie. "Now, give me that paper."

Dinah perched obediently at Aggie's feet and handed her the fresh, crackling newspaper. Aggie glanced through it with little excitement, then turned to the front page. "Here," she barked, tapping a yellowed fingernail on the first paragraph. "Read that word."

Dinah knew the shape of the word well – a short one with a bar through it, a tall one with a curve at the bottom, a little curve with a line in the middle. It was one of the first words she'd learned from Aggie. "The," she said promptly.

"And this one?" said Aggie.

Dinah frowned. The next word was rather long. Sometimes she wondered if it would be easier to learn one letter at a time; did they all make the same sounds all the time? Maybe Aggie didn't know herself. The first three letters looked like the word *sew*. "Sew-er?" she guessed.

"Sewer," Aggie corrected.

"Sewer." Dinah nodded. She knew the next word. "In. White. Street. Is…"

Haltingly, she went on. Aggie, for all her impatience, never seemed to give up with her; and despite her dire threats to stop every few sentences, she helped Dinah get through the entire article. She'd learned a few new words by the end, and as she and Ollie headed back across the hallway to their own tenement with the three little Morris boys in tow, she played them over in her mind. *Sewer. Filth. Stench.* She wasn't sure what a "stench" was, and neither was Aggie, but they both guessed it had something to do with a bad smell.

The tenement she shared with Ollie and her mother was almost identical to the Morris tenement, except the holes in the walls were bigger here. Dinah secreted her newspaper away under the sleeping pallet she shared with Ollie; Mama also slept there, when she was home, and Dinah could only hope that she wouldn't notice the paper. The page she'd already read was wrapped around the fish that Aggie had given her. It was already cooked, and even though it smelled a little strong, Dinah's mouth was watering.

She dispensed it to the little boys, placing their portions into their grubby hands, and nibbled slowly on her own to make it last for as long as possible. When it was all gone, the boys went back to their game while she tipped their last few bits of coal into the stove and struggled with the damp matches to get it to light.

If Mama didn't come back tomorrow, they would have neither coal nor food left. Aggie was kind sometimes, but she didn't have much to go around herself; Dinah knew she couldn't count on the gruff older lady's charity. She couldn't leave Ollie alone.

There was nothing else for it but to hope that Mama came back soon.

MAMA DIDN'T COME BACK that evening.

THE SHAMED LITTLE MATCH GIRL

London was gripped in a cold, noisy darkness. The windows in the tenement were all boarded up, but Dinah could hear rather than see the streets of Whitechapel fading into evening. The shouted arguments from the other tenements grew quieter; caterwauling sounded from the rooftops as stray cats squabbled over what little scraps were left. The shuffle of feet filled the streets as the weary workers trailed home from the factory districts.

Dinah sat on the sleeping pallet, her back against the cold wall, feeling the cold tendrils of the frigid drafts lifting her matted hair and touching her goose-pimpled skin. The little boys were still playing quietly in their corner; the fish had made them sleepy for a while, and they'd woken up with bright eyes and gone back to their little war games. Dinah tried to focus on the second page of the newspaper. It was so hard sometimes to remember the shapes of the words. The third one in the second sentence on this page was appallingly long and difficult: *s-i-t-u-a-t-i-on*. She could puzzle out "sit", but she had no idea what the rest could be.

She was just skipping to the rest of the sentence to see if it held any clues as to the meaning of the mystery word when she heard the familiar squeak of the staircase leading to the top floor. At once, Dinah was on her feet. For a wildly hopeful moment, she thought that it might be Mama, returning at last. But by the time she'd reached the door, she could hear that it was two people coming up the stairs, and a moment later Aggie's two oldest children appeared on the landing.

The moment Dinah met Benjamin Morris' eyes, something stirred deeply inside her, something powerful and unfamiliar that made her feel a little strange. It made her smile without even having to think about it. Maybe it was something about the shade of his eyes: they were forest green, a color that was never a part of life in this tenement or in the whole of Whitechapel; a color that was filled with life and brightness. Dinah had seen a tree on the corner of a street once in full summer, and its rich head of leaves had spoken with a throaty voice when the wind stirred it. When she'd reached out to touch one of the leaves, it had been soft and humming with life. Every time she looked into Benjamin's eyes, she thought of that tree. She thought of the way it grew, strong and steady, its roots running deep, its branches reaching high.

It had been that way ever since the Morrises first moved in next door to the Shaws, when Mama was pregnant with Ollie and Dinah had been only seven years old. Benjamin had been eight then. They'd been friends at once, but these days, Dinah was starting to feel something else stirring between them. It made her shy and excited all at once.

"Benjamin," she said, then added quickly, "Pearl. It's nice to see you."

Benjamin's older sister gave Dinah a wary look. Her eyes were very tired. "Hello, Di," she mumbled. "I'm going to bed."

She pushed the curtain aside and disappeared into the Morris tenement. Benjamin cast Dinah one of those easy smiles of his. She always wondered how he did it; she felt like she had to fight for each smile, to think of every muscle that was needed to lift her lips and crinkle her eyes. Benjamin smiled with his whole face, as if it was something that bubbled up from inside him as naturally as a fresh mountain spring.

"Don't mind her," he said. "It's hard in that match factory. Another one of her friends has died from phossy jaw."

Dinah shuddered at the thought. She'd seen some of the match girls walking in the streets before, tattered scarves bound around their oozing faces. "I'm sorry," she said.

"Me too. Poor Pearl has had enough to worry about ever since Papa left," sighed Benjamin.

"Maybe it's a good thing that I don't know who my papa is," said Dinah. "At least, he couldn't go off and break my heart like yours did."

"He broke all of our hearts," said Benjamin, "but Mama's worst of all. She's never been the same." His eyes grew shadowed for a moment, then brightened. "But let's not talk about that. Is your mama home yet?"

"No," admitted Dinah. "It's been three days."

"Di, that's awful." Benjamin took a step closer, his eyes deepening somehow. "I'll ask Mama if we have a bit of extra food for you."

"She gave us some fish," said Dinah. "She's so good to us, when Mama's not around."

"I don't know why my mother doesn't like yours," said Benjamin. "She won't even let me come over when your mama is home."

Dinah shrugged. She didn't want to tell Benjamin about her horrible suspicions, for though she was only twelve, she wasn't completely ignorant; still, if she did confess her thoughts, maybe Benjamin would look down on her then, the way Aggie looked down on Mama. "Please tell her thanks for the fish," she said. "I don't know what Ollie and I would do without you." She met his eyes. "Without all of you."

"And I don't know what I'd do without you," said Benjamin. "It's good to have someone to talk to."

The hallway was even draftier than the tenement, but Dinah couldn't seem to bring herself to go back inside. "How was your work today?" she asked.

"Well, I didn't get crushed by a horse," said Benjamin, laughing.

"Don't joke, Benji." Dinah shuddered. "It's happened to so many of the boys who pick up manure like you do."

"Oh, don't worry. I'm careful," said Benjamin. "And I like it, actually. I like watching the horses. I'm getting to know what they look like when they're going to be nervous or try to kick out. The old heavy horses are the best; they never startle even if you scoop the manure right out from under their feet."

His eyes were shining, and Dinah was marveling again at the way he could always find good things in the midst of everything, even a task as dirty and dangerous as cleaning manure from the busy London streets. She wished she could tell him how much she admired him; yet looking into his eyes, she couldn't seem to find the words.

The silence grew awkward. Dinah stepped back, feeling her cheeks burning. "Well, I'm glad you had a good day," she said. "I... I'll call the boys."

"Thank you for looking after them," said Benjamin.

The tone of his voice and the way he leaned forward made Dinah feel like he had more to say, but she felt too flustered to keep talking with him, even if it was the one thing she wanted to do most in all the world. She opened the squeaky door of her tenement and called, "Bobby, Job, Aaron— Benjamin's here for you."

The little ones rushed over to Benjamin, shouting, their arms held out to him. Ollie was among them; they giggled and clutched at his clothes as he swept them into his arms one by one, laughing and tickling them. For a few glorious moments, the tenement hallway echoed with the laughter of happy children.

And it was all because of Benjamin.

OLLIE WAS a warm bundle in Dinah's arms. She curled herself around him, cuddling his little body as close as she could for warmth. The dim red glow from the coal stove cast deep shadows under his black curls; they lay in oily ringlets on his cheeks, and he had his thumb in his mouth. Mama hated it when Ollie sucked his thumb, but Dinah couldn't bring herself to make him stop.

She brushed some of the curls out of his face and pulled their single blanket more snugly around both of their shoulders. He breathed slowly and deeply, his pink lips working around his thumb as he sucked it for comfort. Dinah felt a warm, fierce affection deep in her heart, tinged with desperation. It had been a whole day since Aggie gave them the fish; Ollie had cried himself to sleep with hunger. There were two pale tracks running down the dirt on his face where the tears had trickled down.

Mama had to come back. As always, Dinah felt a cold, dreadful fear rise in her: a fear that Mama would never come, that the great, hungry city had swallowed her the way it swallowed so many other souls. It was like some predatory beast – never satiated, always seeking to devour someone right out of Dinah's life, the way it had devoured Benjamin's father.

She wrapped her arms more tightly around Ollie and buried her face in his curls. It couldn't be. Mama had to come back. She always came back, even though this time she'd been gone for five days. She'd never been gone for five days before. But she would come back.

She had to.

Somehow, among the whirl of frightened thoughts and the ache of hunger in Dinah's belly, she managed to find her way into a restless sleep. She seldom slept deeply; the creaks and whistles of the old building shaking around them, Ollie's twitches as he dreamed, and the cold draft that never stopped blowing on her back were constantly plucking her back from real sleep. Tonight was no exception. She faltered in an uncomfortable doze, always aware of the biting cold.

Somewhere in the senseless world of half-wake, half-sleep, a bolt slammed. Dinah jerked awake. She sat up quickly, pulling the blanket off Ollie by accident; he stirred, mumbled, his smooth little brow furrowing. Dinah tugged the blanket back around his shoulders without thinking. She listened, trembling. Had she dreamed it, or did it sound like someone had just bolted the big main door at the bottom of the building? The walls were so thin that even three stories up, she could always hear it.

No. She hadn't dreamed it. There were footsteps coming up the stairs now. Dinah reached for the bit of broken plank that had come out of their door, thinking of the strange men that loitered on the corners of the streets outside. They had funny eyes – twitchy and rheumy – and lately Dinah had been noticing more and more often how those eyes followed her whenever she walked with Mama and Ollie. She tightened her grip on the plank. It was a little splintery, but with enough desperation behind it, it would do for a weapon.

The footsteps were coming closer now, reaching the second floor. Dinah slipped off the pallet and padded to the door, her heart hammering. Should she call for Benjamin? But what could he do? He was the man of the house, but he was only thirteen, and hardly any bigger than she was. Still, she wanted the warmth of him beside her when she faced whoever it was that had just reached the top floor. Dinah cowered against the doorway, her heart racing as she clutched the plank, and any thought of summoning help had fled from her mind. She remembered an article she'd read with Aggie not long ago, about someone they called Jack the Ripper, and her stomach turned very cold. She hoped now that whatever-it-was would simply go away and think that this tenement was abandoned, instead of coming inside here and doing something awful...

There was a shove at the door. Dinah had her shoulder pressed against it, and she just managed to hold back a squeal of terror. She leaned into it instead, her heart pounding.

"Dinah?" said a voice.

A sudden wave of relief washed over her. She jumped back, dropping the plank with a clatter, and pulled the door wide open. "Mama," she cried.

Mama stood in the doorway, her eyes – so like Ollie's – two great hollows in her pale face. Her white-blonde hair hung in strands around her face, so long that it reached all the way to her hips. When Dinah was little, she had always believed that there couldn't possibly be anyone in the world as beautiful as her mother; Mama was like something magical, like a sprite or some faerie spirit. Yet the passage of the years had been as unkind to Mama's looks as they had been to Dinah's perspective. Now, Mama's long hair hugged her like a tattered shroud. Her deep eyes were no longer whimsical, but hollow. They watched Dinah without interest now, and Dinah noticed that

Mama's willowy figure was clad in yet another new dress. She'd long since stopped believing that Mama got these new dresses from friendly ladies in the street, especially given how far down the necklines always seemed to go over Mama's rail-thin chest.

"You're home," said Dinah, unable to hide her relief. She knew better than to hug Mama, even though her arms ached to do it. Mama never wanted to be touched – not even by Ollie – when she'd just come home from a few days of... work.

"Yes," said Mama. "I'm cold."

Dinah stepped back. Her mother floated into the room, her emaciation unable to rob her of her elegance. Dinah closed the door behind her, and Mama sat down on the sleeping pallet. Ollie, deep in the innocent sleep of a small child, didn't move.

"Are you hungry?" Dinah asked, knowing that there was no food in the house.

Mama was never hungry when she returned. She was just tired. "No," she said. She rummaged in the folds of her dress and pulled out a little cloth pouch of money, pushing it across the floor to Dinah. "Pay the rent," she said.

"Thank you, Mama," said Dinah.

Mama said nothing. She just lay down beside Ollie, laid one hand on the child's shoulder, and closed her eyes.

CHAPTER 2

Mornings after Mama returned were always some of Dinah's happiest times, and especially so when they happened to be Sunday mornings. Mama never wanted much to do with Dinah and Ollie when she'd just gotten back; she just wanted to sleep, and feebly spoon up whatever soup Dinah made. It was up to Dinah to go out to the market and buy food and coal, but she never minded, for this was the one time that she was able to see the outside world. And this time, since it was a Sunday morning, Benjamin was with them.

Walking through the streets of Whitechapel was never particularly pleasant, especially on a snowy morning in January with the vengeful wind throwing blinding sleet against Dinah's face like tiny arrows. The snow was falling hard and thick on top of grimy mud and yellowed slush, churning into the unpaved road by the passage of foot traffic and the occasional donkey cart. The lurking men on the shadowy corners were still there, and their eyes still followed Dinah in a way that made her clutch Ollie's hand very tightly. But with Benjamin by her side, she felt more at ease.

He was singing this morning; he sang often, and he had a fine, powerful voice that echoed through their entire tenement sometimes when Aggie wasn't too irritated to let him sing. Now, there was no one to stop him, and his voice resounded in the gloom.

"Lavender blue, dilly dilly," he sang. "Lavender green. When I am king, dilly dilly, you shall be queen." He flashed Dinah a smile that sent an unexpected jolt of warmth through her body.

"Thank you for coming with us." Dinah smiled into the contented silence once he'd finished his song. "I know your mama wasn't very happy about it."

"Mama doesn't mind. She just doesn't want me to be near your mother," said Benjamin, shrugging. "But let's not talk about our silly mothers now. We're going to the market. What are we going to buy?"

"Food," cried Ollie. "Vegetables and potatoes and fish and beef."

"Well, maybe a little bit of tripe," said Dinah. "And some turnips."

"And milk?" said Ollie hopefully.

"No, darling," said Dinah. "Even if we could afford milk, we wouldn't have anywhere to keep it."

Ollie pouted, but only briefly. The moment he set his eyes on the market square, his face lit up, and he started tugging at Dinah's hand to look at every stall. Even to Dinah, the square was a little magical. Poverty was still evident in every line and curve of the scene before her: the stalls were made with sticks bound together to hold up old rags for a little shelter from the snow, the wares placed out on old boxes or planks held up by two broken barrels instead of tables. But there was so much to see, so many people bustling in every direction. Shiny silver fish lay in neat rows on the tables. Jars of jam and pickled vegetables, piles of bright carrots, live chickens clucking in makeshift cages – the entire square buzzed with life. Vendors cried their wares against the wind, shoppers wandered among the stalls, and pickpockets stared from shady corners, their sharp eyes quick to spot the glitter of a pocket-watch chain. Dinah kept her money gripped tightly in both hands.

"It's all right." Benjamin laid his hand over hers, noticing her worry. "I'm here. No one's going to take that."

Dinah relaxed a little, smiling up at him. "You're very useful, Benji," she said.

He gave her a gallant little bow. "I try my best."

Benjamin carried a hessian sack that Dinah always used when she was shopping, and Mama had brought back plenty of money this time – probably because she'd been gone for so long. Dinah was able to fill the sack with potatoes, fish wrapped in newspaper, carrots, beets that had gone only slightly moldy, a heavy parcel of tripe, and enough coal to last them a week. There was still enough money left for rent, she noted with relief. She didn't want to think about what would happen if Mama someday didn't come back soon enough to pay rent of a Monday morning.

There was even a few extra pennies to buy three fresh loaves of bread, which Dinah gave to Benjamin. He protested at first, but only a little. He was just as hungry as Dinah.

They walked home slowly, after eating the watery soup filled with questionable green bits and gristle that they'd purchased from a hunchbacked old lady on the street corner. The snow had stopped, and a shy ray of sunshine was poking its tentative head through the clouds, just enough to glitter modestly on the newly fallen snow. Ollie ran on ahead; Dinah kept her eyes on him, but the streets were fairly empty this close to home, and she didn't have the heart to stop him from taking his chance to run and play.

"Tell me," said Benjamin, tearing another chunk off the loaf of bread. "What do you want to do one day when you're grown up?"

Dinah laughed. "Oh, Benji, you and your funny questions." she said.

"No, I'm serious." Benjamin smiled.

Dinah didn't normally like to think of the future. It felt like standing at the top of some very steep slope, with a dark abyss at the bottom. Still, with the sunlight on Benjamin's full head of red waves, and his smile warming her heart, she decided she'd humor him this time. "I don't know," she said. "Going to bed with a full belly every night would be a good start."

"Oh, come on, Dinah." Benjamin grinned. "You must have a little more than that in you."

Dinah paused. Ollie was some way ahead now; she lowered her voice a little. "I suppose I want to be able to read," she said softly. "I want Ollie to have a good future – to get an education and have a good position in life. And I don't want to be like my mother."

Benjamin studied her. "Why not?" he asked softly.

Dinah turned her head away. "I don't know," she finally admitted, "but whatever she does, I don't want to do that."

"Isn't she a flower seller?" Benjamin asked.

Dinah sighed and only said, "I don't think so."

He must have sensed the weight behind her words, for he changed the subject quickly. "I want to do something with horses," he said firmly. "I want to have a beautiful stable of my own. Or maybe I'll be a cab driver. Or even a stable master."

Dinah laughed. "I think you'll have a stable of your own one day," she said. "With all the horses you could ever want."

Benjamin smiled. And with all of her heart, Dinah hoped that her words would come true. Benjamin deserved so much better than this.

They all did.

THE NEXT MORNING, Dinah stood in the doorway of their tenement, a few bright coins clutched tightly in her fist. She could hear the dreaded thump of Reuben Scully's feet as he moved around on the second floor, hear the gruff, oily bubble of his voice below. Their landlord never came to the tenement building except for rent, and Dinah was glad of it. Once, when she was very small, Aggie had tried to demand that Scully repair the door to her tenement. Scully had slapped Aggie so hard across the face that she'd fallen backward through the door, snapping the rotten wood right through the middle and breaking two of her fingers in her fall. She had never asked again. No one asked him anything; they just paid their rent and didn't make a fuss.

For the last few years, the task had fallen to Dinah. Mama was still fast asleep on the pallet; Ollie was curled up beside her, a little bundle of warmth at her back. Dinah shivered in the drafty hallway, longing to join them.

Scully's feet were coming up the stairs now, and Dinah shot a glance at the curtain to the Morris tenement. Where was Aggie? Pearl and Benjamin had long since gone off to work; she could hear the voices of the three little brothers as they played. But there was no sign of Aggie.

An awful fear had just started to rise in Dinah's belly when Scully stepped into the hallway. As always, Dinah felt everything inside her cringe at the sight of their landlord. He was a short fellow with bandy legs and a round belly, but this did not serve to make him any less threatening. His black hair was slicked back with oily efficiency; his clothes were much too tight, the collar of his shirt nipping right into his fleshy neck. He had small, quick hands with little fat fingers. He would have been a funny little figure, perhaps even jolly, if it wasn't for two things: his mouth and his eyes. His eyes were very dark and flat, set wide apart and too shallow, like a shark's. And he never stopped smiling. It was a terrifying expression, wide and steady, showing off two rows of very white teeth.

He was doing it now as he walked toward Dinah, those predatory eyes sweeping over her. "Well, well, little Miss Shaw," he said.

"G-good morning, sir," said Dinah. She cleared her throat quickly, holding out her fist. "I've got your money."

"Now there's a little girl who knows what's good for her." Scully held out a hand. Dinah dropped the money into it quickly, careful not to let her fingertips touch his skin; his hands were white and looked very clammy. "Is your mother in?" he asked, arching an eyebrow.

Dinah hesitated. She hated the opportunistic slant that had come to Scully's face. "No, sir," she said. "She left this morning."

For a moment, Scully's shark eyes bored into Dinah's, and she feared he might push past her and see for himself. Instead, there was a rustle behind him, and Aggie said, "Here's your rent, sir."

Scully turned. If Aggie was afraid of him after the blow he'd given her all those years ago, she didn't show it. There was steady defiance in her eyes as she held out her hand.

"Ah, Mrs. Morris," said Scully, his voice slipping over Dinah's skin—as smooth and sticky as oil.

"Don't you 'Mrs. Morris' me," growled Aggie. "Take your money and go. Leave the child alone."

"Oh, don't you worry, Agatha." Scully gave a dark, slithery chuckle. "It'll be a few more years before I intend to truly bother her."

Aggie gave him a furious look, and Scully held out his hand, meeting her eyes. Her upper lip twitched, and she dropped the money into his palm. He studied it for a second, then flashed her an angry look. "You know as well as I do that your rent is more than that."

"It's been a bad week. Bobby had a fever. I bought him medicine," said Aggie coolly. "Benjamin and Pearl will bring back wages again on Saturday. You'll have the rest of your money next week."

"Next week?" Scully's voice dropped an octave. "You think you can pay me late, Agatha?"

"I'll pay interest," said Aggie.

"Interest." Scully laughed. "As if you even know what interest is, you stupid old hag."

Aggie took a step forward, her shoulders expanding to her full height, a sudden reminder that she was several inches taller than Scully. Her rheumy eyes were on fire now. "What are you going to do?" she thundered. "Evict me?"

Scully's face paled. He took a step back, clutching the money she'd given him, and rage burned in his cold eyes. "Don't make me do it," he growled, his voice high-pitched with rage and fear. "Don't test me, Agatha."

She folded her arms. "I'll see you next week. You'll get your money," she snapped.

Scully bared his teeth in something that was more of a snarl than a smile. "Oh yes," he said icily. "You know that I will."

He stormed away, stomping down the wobbly stairs, and Aggie closed her eyes. She leaned against the doorframe as if the effort of shouting at Scully had drained the last of her energy. Dinah rushed over to her, grabbing her hands. "Aggie," she gasped.

"Don't make a fuss, child." Agatha pulled her hands out of Dinah's.

"Are you all right?" Dinah asked.

Aggie sighed. "I will be," she said. "Go back to your mother now, there's a good girl. Everything is all right."

Dinah backed away. But as she watched Aggie limping back into her tenement, she wasn't so sure.

THE SHAMED LITTLE MATCH GIRL

BY WEDNESDAY, Mama was gone again. Dinah woke to a sleeping pallet that felt cold in Mama's absence, and to a silent tenement. Her first feeling was one of abrupt relief. At least now she didn't have to feed all three of them from the stock of food they'd bought at the market on Sunday.

Her second was guilt. How could she be glad that her mama was gone? But ever since Dinah was little, she'd known that Mama was not the same thing to her and Ollie that Aggie was to Benjamin and the others. Aggie was gruff and scolded the children often, but she cooked for them and put them to bed. Mama, when she was home, did little more than sleep. Sometimes Dinah wondered if she and Ollie needed her at all – except for the money. Of course, they needed that. It was all that stood between them and starvation.

She warmed up a little gruel for breakfast and took Ollie to the Morris tenement. Aggie was in a foul mood; she refused to help Dinah with the reading and seemed on the brink of another runny-nosed, feverish cold. Dinah swept her floors and made soup for the children, which seemed to soothe Aggie's temper a little. When Benjamin and Pearl returned from work, they ate the runny soup with a few turnips thrown in from Dinah's stores, and then Dinah and Benjamin sat in a corner and talked in hushed voices until everyone was asleep.

"When do you think your mother will come back?" Benjamin asked softly.

Dinah shrugged. "She never used to go away for longer than three days. But last time, she was gone for five," she said. "We've got enough food to last us for about six days. A week, if we stretch it thinly."

They sat in silence for a few moments. The fire in Aggie's stove snapped gently.

"I don't know how you do it," said Benjamin softly.

"What?" asked Dinah.

"Well – *anything*, without your mother," said Benjamin. "I wouldn't be able to sleep in that dark, quiet tenement without Mama." His eyes lit on Aggie, and deep love flickered in them.

"Mama's not the same as your mother," said Dinah softly.

"I know." Benjamin smiled. "You are, though."

"I am what?" asked Dinah, laughing.

"You're like my mama. Not so grumpy, of course." Benjamin chuckled. "And prettier. But you wouldn't leave your children either. Not for anything in the world."

Dinah thought of Ollie, and that fierce thing roared in her heart again.

"No," she said. "You're right about that."

༻✦༺

THREE DAYS CAME AND WENT. Then the weekend, and on Monday morning, there was still no sign of Mama.

Dinah was trembling from head to toe as she stood in the door of the tenement. Any minute now, Scully was going to come through that doorway, and she was going to hand over the precious few coins she'd earned from selling the last of their food to one of the families that lived on the second floor. There was nothing left now. It was a choice that had grown horribly familiar to Dinah: she could either have a home to stay in, or food on the table. And with the January wind wailing around the corners of the ramshackle building, its voice shrill and pitiful, she knew that it would be easier to survive a few days without food than a single night without shelter.

The coins slipped around in her sweaty palm, and she tightened her grip over them as she listened to Scully coming up the steps. She wished Benjamin was home. She'd feel so much braver facing Scully with him by her side, and she'd gotten up early that morning to wait by the door in the hopes that she could just see his face and hear his cheery voice as he passed down the hall on his way to work. But he must have left even earlier than she'd woken; he never came down the hall. Now her feet had gone numb and her knees were stiff from standing in the drafty hall. She tried not to think about how hungry she was already, or how hungry she would be at this time tomorrow morning.

Oh, Mama. Dinah squeezed her eyes shut. *Where are you?*

"Well, hello, little Miss Shaw."

Dinah jumped, almost dropping the coins in her hand. Scully was walking down the hall toward her, smiling in his oily way, his flat eyes staring at her. "Is your mama still not home?" he said.

Dinah forced a smile. "She was, but she's gone again," she said.

"Oh, well. That means I'll be getting my money from you, at least," growled Sculley.

Dinah held out her hand. "Yes, sir. It's all there."

"Good." Scully chuckled as he snatched the coins from Dinah. "I'd hate to evict your mama without having the pleasure of being one of her customers."

His chuckle felt so sticky and dirty that Dinah wanted to wash out her ears after hearing it. She decided not to say anything and stepped back, her eyes on the curtain to the Morris tenement. There was no one there, and an awful fear started to grow in Dinah's belly.

"Now," grumbled Scully, "where is that no-good old hag?"

The curtain swept aside. "Don't call my mama a hag," snapped Benjamin.

Dinah gave an involuntary gasp. She hadn't been expecting Benjamin, and the sight of him in a fine fury – his cheeks bright red, his green eyes ablaze – was enough to set her heart racing. But what really frightened her was the tone of voice he'd used with Scully. His jaw clenched as he stepped out into the hallway.

"Young Mr. Morris," said Scully, his voice low and threatening. "I'll call your mother whatever I please until she pays her rent. I've already given her more grace than she deserves."

"My mama deserves all the good things this world could ever give her," growled Benjamin.

"Benji, please." Aggie stepped out from behind the curtain and took Benjamin's arm. "Just give Mr. Scully his money."

Dinah's shoulders sagged with relief. She'd had a terrible feeling that the Morrises weren't able to pay their rent. Benjamin still had a dangerous glint in his eye, but he relented, reaching into his pocket. "Here, sir," he said, handing over some money.

Scully counted it with a single glance, which he then leveled at Benjamin like some kind of weapon. "Do you take me for a fool, boy?" he barked.

"It's the rent," said Benjamin. "Same as always."

"Yes, now, that's the problem." Scully thundered. "Your mother here gave me her word that she would pay me back the rent she owes me for last week."

"Mr. Scully, please." Aggie stepped forward, putting a hand on the seething Benjamin's arm. "I'll have it next week."

"What's your excuse this time?" Scully barked.

"The baker was out of stale bread when we went to buy food. We had to buy fresh. We didn't have a choice," Aggie pleaded. "I have to feed my children. You know that."

Dinah stared in horror. She'd never seen Aggie beg so humbly before.

"Please, sir. What would you have me do?" said Aggie, and then she repeated, "I have to feed my children."

"You have to pay your debt, you little witch," barked Scully. He planted his hands on his hips. "I've had about enough of your nonsense and your lies, Agatha."

"We'll have it next week," said Benjamin, stepping forward. "Please, just give us some time."

"Hold your tongue, boy." Scully shook an angry fist under Benjamin's nose. "I put this roof over your ungrateful heads. Do you know what a fortune it costs to keep this place up and running? Why, I barely make a bent penny on you people, and you still insist on throwing my charity back in my face."

"Charity?" Benjamin cried. "Charity? You make no repairs to this place. You treat us all like scum under your feet." He took a step forward, bringing himself nose to nose with Scully. Dinah realized abruptly that Benjamin was taller than their landlord. "And you dare to even speak the word 'charity'."

Scully's eyes grew flat and dark, the way they did before he did something terrible. "Mind your tone, boy," he hissed, one hand going to his pocket. Dinah didn't want to think about what he was grasping there.

"Please just leave," said Benjamin, his voice trembling. "We'll pay you as soon as we can."

"Oh, I don't think so," snapped Scully. "You'll pay me now, or you'll get out of my house."

Benjamin's eyes widened in desperation. Dinah wished she hadn't already given Scully her money. She would have given anything, even the clothes off her back, at that moment to wipe away the utter terror she saw in Benjamin's eyes. For a long instant, Benjamin's hands curled into fists, and Dinah thought he might strike Scully right where he stood.

But it was only an instant. Benjamin's shoulders sagged, and his face was lined with defeat.

"We don't have the money," he said flatly.

"Then get out," hissed Scully.

"No!" The shriek came from Aggie. She lunged forward, her desperation echoing around the hallway. "One week, Scully," she shrieked, storming toward him. "One week. You can't give us one week, you mongrel?"

"Mama, no!" shouted Benjamin.

With Aggie storming down on him, Scully had jerked his hand out of his pocket, and Dinah just had enough time to see the ugly little club in his hand before he was raising it over his head at Aggie. Benjamin reached for her, grasping her arm with both hands, yanking her back to safety as the club whistled through the air. Dinah was running before she could think. As Scully stumbled with the force of his blow, she reached him, both arms outstretched, and slammed her hands into his shoulder.

Scully stumbled backwards for a few wobbling steps before falling. He flung out his hands to catch himself, the club skittering away across the floorboards as he landed heavily on his hands and rump. Unhurt but irate, he glared up at them all, and they froze in the face of his rage.

His eyes landed on Dinah, and she felt them slice through her like some icy blade. "You," he growled, rising to his feet.

"Please, sir, I can help," said Dinah, her heart hammering. "I can help them get their money. Please. You know Mama makes good money. You know she'll come back with some. I'll pay you their rent. I'll help them. Please, please, sir, don't evict them."

Scully stared at her. "Do you think I care?" he roared, stepping toward her. "There are millions of people in this city looking for a tenement – people who will pay for it."

"But sir, they need their home," Dinah begged. "Oh, sir, please, don't you have a heart?"

"No!" Benjamin cried.

It was too late. Scully had already drawn back his hand and delivered a ringing blow across Dinah's cheekbone. She staggered back, falling to the floor, a hand raised to her burning cheek.

Benjamin started toward her. Scully swung around, raising a threatening fist. "Don't," he roared. "Don't take a single step. Get back into that tenement, pack your things, and get out of my house." He spat on the floor. "Before I call my friend in the police to make you do it."

Benjamin's eyes rested on Dinah, and she had never seen them so sad, so filled with anguish.

She knew they had all been beaten, but it was too hard to see it in Benjamin's face. So she turned her eyes away and wept as Scully stormed off, and the Morrises slunk back through the curtain to the home they had just lost.

CHAPTER 3

"Benjamin?" Dinah whispered.

Her cheek was still throbbing from Scully's blow. Ollie had looked terrified when she'd stumbled back into her tenement and he'd seen the rising, red swelling, but she'd managed to sing him back to sleep. Now she huddled in the doorway of their tenement, listening to the strained voices and crying children from the room across the hall.

Benjamin had just emerged. His eyes were very red, and he hadn't bothered to wipe away the tears on his cheeks. Dinah imagined that the cloth bag he carried in one hand contained most of the Morrises' worldly possessions. A few pots and pans. The battered old Bible Aggie always carried. Perhaps a cup or two, and a few wooden forks, and a blunt knife.

"Oh, Dinah." Benjamin's anguished face crumpled even further when he saw her. He put down the bag and came over to her, crouching down in front of her. "I'm so sorry."

It took Dinah a moment to realize that he was talking about the bruise on her cheek. "It's all right," she said. "What will you do now? Where will you go?"

"Well, Pearl and I still have our jobs." Benjamin took a shaky breath. "I'm sure we'll find somewhere to stay." He gave her a smile that wasn't sure at all; a sad, watery version of his usual dazzling grin.

"But where?" Dinah whispered. "And will I ever see you again?"

Benjamin's eyes were glittering with tears. "I don't know," he whimpered, and they began to flow down his cheeks unchecked. "I don't know, Dinah." A sob bubbled up from deep within him. "I don't want to go," he cried.

His anguish was more than Dinah could bear. It felt like her heart was being torn to pieces. She wrapped her arms around him, feeling him tremble, and hugged him as tightly as she could. She bowed her face down into his hair and let it absorb her own tears, and their weeping echoed around the hallway, making it sound like its very walls were full of mourning ghosts.

"Benji." It was Aggie's voice. Dinah looked up to see her gently grasping Benjamin's arm. "It's time to go, love."

Dinah didn't want to let him go. She wanted to hold on to him forever, but already he was slipping out of her arms, wiping his eyes on his grubby sleeve. He gave her a haunted look as he picked up the bag, but he didn't say anything. Aggie tried to smile for Dinah. "Keep reading," she said.

"I'll never stop," Dinah whispered.

They turned away, the three little boys utterly subdued, drooping in a row behind their mother. Pearl walked ahead, her back very straight, her chin lifted. Benjamin brought up the rear. Dinah watched him until he reached the door, and then she couldn't contain it anymore.

"Benjamin!" she cried, getting to her feet.

He turned. She had so much that she wanted to say. So many feelings that she couldn't name. She wanted to tell him that he was the only real joy in her life, that the tenement building would feel like a prison without him, that the world would feel colorless without the shade of his eyes. But none of it would come out.

"Goodbye," she whispered instead.

Benjamin managed a wan smile.

"Until we meet again," he murmured, and then he was gone.

OLLIE'S CRIES rang through the empty tenement. Dinah thought it must be her imagination, but somehow his weeping sounded a thousand times louder and more echoing now that the Morris tenement was empty. He lay face-down on the dirty floor, his curls spilling into the grime that covered the floorboards, his clenched little fists slamming into the floor again and again as his wide-open mouth emitted one gut-wrenching wail after the other.

Dinah sat on the sleeping pallet, staring at him. She'd spent all day trying to find ways to keep him busy, to keep his mind off the fact that they had eaten nothing for more than a day now, but it wasn't working. Slowly Ollie had been spiraling out of control, and with every shrill cry, Dinah could feel her own courage and empathy wearing away. Her belly ached constantly with pangs of growing hunger; her heart felt much worse, like it had been pulled out of her chest and run over by a steam train. Outside, the wind howled. Inside, the drafts were freezing.

"I'm hungry," Ollie screeched, slamming his fists into the floor. "I'm so hungry."

Dinah gritted her teeth and covered her face with her hands, trying to find some hidden well of strength. But this time, thinking of Benjamin only made it worse.

"I want Bobby and Aaron and Job," Ollie howled. "I want them back. Bring them back."

Dinah knew, in her mind, that Ollie was only five and didn't understand why she couldn't do as he demanded. Still, the helplessness his words evoked in her made something snap. She got to her feet and stormed over to him, grabbing him by his arm.

"Get up!" she shouted at him.

"No. I'm too hungry," Ollie wailed.

"Do you think you're the only one that's hungry?" She yanked Ollie to his feet, glaring into his eyes. "Do you think you're the only one missing your friends?"

He stared at her, wide-eyed.

"Stop your racket right now," Dinah bellowed. "I'm tired of it. Stop it. I can't listen to this anymore."

Ollie's face crumpled, his brown eyes burning with genuine pain. Dinah had only a moment to feel remorse before he flung back his head and started screaming again, his mouth wide. She let go of his arm and took a deep breath, preparing for more yelling, when the sound of the door opening behind them silenced them both instantly.

Dinah spun around. Mama stood in the doorway, and Dinah felt a wave of delicious relief wash over her when she saw the familiar little money pouch clutched in Mama's hand. Then she let it go. The pouch thumped down onto the floor with a dull, clinking sound, and when Dinah looked up into Mama's eyes, they were unnaturally bright in her deathly pale face.

Something about the hue of Mama's skin made Dinah's heart stand quite still. Her voice came out small and frightened, very different from the roar she'd just given Ollie.

"M-Mama?"

Mama let out a breath that was somewhere between a sigh and a sob. Her delicate legs crumpled underneath her, and she slipped gently to the floor, sprawling on the filthy surface in her pretty new red dress that allowed her chest and shoulders to spill out onto the dirt like milk.

Dinah felt her heart squeeze. She rushed to her mother. "Mama!" she cried.

Ollie was sobbing again – not the tantrum cry he'd used a minute ago, but a quieter, more desperate sound as he grabbed Mama's hand and clung to it. Dinah touched her shoulder; it was blazing with heat, as if she'd just pressed her fingers to the stove. She grasped Mama's shoulder and rolled her over, bending anxiously over her face.

"Mama. Mama. Mama," Ollie sobbed.

"She's breathing," said Dinah, feeling her hands shake as she placed them on Mama's face. "But she's burning with fever."

"Is she sick?" Ollie turned a tear-streaked face toward her.

"I... I think so," said Dinah.

"Is she going to die?" asked Ollie.

Dinah met his eyes, his terrified eyes, and her heart froze. That wasn't an option. Mama's money was the only thing keeping them alive.

"No," she said, although she wasn't sure she believed it. "Come on. Let's get her to the pallet."

She threaded her arms under Mama's shoulders and lifted, surprised that someone so wispy could be so heavy. As she dragged her to the pallet, she could think of only one thing: how desperately she wished that Benjamin was here.

***

Dinah watched a tiny eddy of snowflakes swirl across the floorboards. They had blown in through a new gap in the wall; a piece of mortar had been broken off there when Dinah had dragged Mama onto the pallet. That had been two days ago – three days ago? Dinah had lost track – and yet it felt like an eternity.

Dinah felt like she had always been here by her mother's bedside, kneeling on the floor, drenching a rag in some cool water and placing it on Mama's forehead, then running it over her burning arms. She couldn't think of anything else to do. She didn't dare to leave Mama alone for too long, so she had bought their meals from the old lady on the street corner who sold bits of stale bread and bowls of questionable stew at three times the price of the vendors on market day. It had kept them alive, but the money in the little pouch was dwindling quickly, and Dinah knew that she would barely be able to feed them and pay the rent with what was left. There was no question of fetching a doctor.

She dipped her rag in the tepid water again, ignoring its dirty, murky look, and gripped Mama's wrist gently to lift her arm.

Her pulse bounded against Dinah's fingers. She didn't know if that was a good or bad thing. She didn't know anything except that Mama's skin was still blazing with heat as she ran the wet rag down the length of her arm, and that she had only woken a few times to drink tiny spoonfuls of soup before drifting back again to some murky land between sleep and death.

Death. Dinah didn't want to think about it. She couldn't. She couldn't bring her mind to imagine what would happen to her and Ollie the day that she could no longer pay Scully.

Tears stung her eyes as she lay the cool cloth over Mama's forehead and sat down again, watching her mother breathe. If only Benjamin could sit here beside her, she would feel better. If only Aggie could watch Ollie, he would stop crying. If only Pearl could go to the market for them, they would have enough money for the doctor.

She closed her eyes, remembering that lovely market day with Benjamin and Ollie, with its weak sunshine and Benjamin's world-changing smile. She remembered him asking, *What do you want to do one day when you're all grown up?*

Dinah lowered her head, biting back her tears so that she wouldn't wake Ollie with them. Right now, she wasn't sure that she would live to be all grown up at all.

Ollie mumbled in his sleep and turned over beside Mama, one curl tumbling over his closed eyes, his chubby fist close to his mouth. A flame rose in her. *No.* She had to live, if only for a few more years. She had to find a way to give Ollie a better life than this.

She gathered what little was left of her courage and soaked the rag in the bucket again. Somehow, she was going to keep her mother alive.

Whatever it took.

⁂

"Is your mother home?"

Dinah was starting to hate the way that Scully asked the question every single Monday. Since he'd walked up the hall to collect the rent – from her and from the drunken old man that now lived in the tenement opposite – Dinah had been too afraid to raise her eyes to Scully's. The bruise on her cheek had gone from black to blue to yellow, but she felt as though it was throbbing again now as she shook her head mutely, dropping the coins into Scully's greasy palm.

Suddenly, Sculley grasped at her wrist. His touch was shockingly cold and damp, and Dinah gasped, stepping back.

"Don't fight me, girl," he growled, squeezing harder. "Do you take me for a fool? Your mother can't always be away. How are you getting your money?"

Dinah raised her eyes, trembling. "I'm s-sorry," she managed. "I m-meant to say that she's home, but she can't see anyone. She's sick. Very sick."

Scully's eyes flickered with vague disappointment, but no compassion. He stepped back, letting go of her hand with a sneer. "Ah, well. I'll see her next week," he hissed, turned around and stalked down the hall.

Dinah let out a long sigh of relief, leaning against the doorframe with her head hanging. An awful wave of fear threatened to break over her head, to engulf her in its cold, drowning embrace. What was she going to say to him next week? Would Mama be well enough to work again by then?

Would they still have a mama, next week?

She gazed listlessly at the curtain across the hall. If Benjamin was here, he would be able to help her. Aggie would give them food and advice. Maybe even some medicine. But there was no one now; no one but Dinah, and Ollie, and a Mama burning with fever.

She turned away and stepped into the tenement, and a ripple of shock ran through her. Mama's eyes were open. They met Dinah's the moment she stepped through the door, and Dinah froze, taking in Mama's clear, steady gaze.

Then Mama spoke. "I'm thirsty," she said.

"Oh, Mama." Dinah ran to her, unable to hold back her cry of joy. She threw her arms around Mama's shoulder, hugging her skinny frame tight. "Oh, Mama, Mama, you're awake."

"I'm thirsty," Mama said again.

Dinah grabbed a tin cup and filled it quickly with water. Mama drank it at once, then another, and finally another before her thirst was slaked. Then she leaned back against the wall, as if the mere effort of drinking the water had drained her of her strength. Still, Dinah could see that the fever was broken; a healthy sweat glittered on Mama's upper lip, and her cheeks had lost that unnatural pallor. She gently touched Mama's arm and found her skin to be cool to the touch at last.

"You're better," Dinah whispered.

Mama gave her something that could have been a smile. "Did you pay Scully?"

"Yes. He was just here."

"It's still Monday. Good," said Mama. She leaned her head back against the wall and ran a hand through Ollie's curls; he was still asleep beside her. "I'll go back tomorrow. Then I'll have money again before he comes for the rent next week."

"Tomorrow?" cried Dinah, dismayed. "But Mama, look at you. You're still weak. You're still *sick*."

"We need the money, Dinah," said Mama firmly. "What else would you have me do?"

"You can't, Mama. You can't go back… there," said Dinah, her heart hammering. "Listen to the wind outside. It's freezing cold. You won't last the walk out of Whitechapel."

Mama glared at her. "What choice do we have, Dinah? We need money." She glanced down at Ollie again.

Dinah squared her shoulders, gaining strength from the soft curve of her brother's cheek, the flutter of his sleeping eyelashes against his skin. "I'll go out and work," she said.

"What are you talking about?" snapped Mama.

"I'll find work. In the factories, like Pearl and Benjamin," said Dinah. A glorious possibility rose in her mind. "Maybe I'll even meet one of them at the factory," she said. "I could find them again."

"What are you talking about?" barked Mama.

"The Morrises were evicted, Mama," said Dinah. "But if I go to work in the factories, I can bring us money, and maybe I'll find them again."

Mama turned her face away. "I don't want you working in the match factory," she spat. "You'll have phossy jaw and die just like all the others."

"Pearl doesn't," said Dinah with determination. Nothing scared her now, not compared with the hope of finding Benjamin again. "And she's been working there for years."

"Dinah..."

"Mama." Dinah took Mama's hand and squeezed it. "Please. You know you can't work in this condition. It'll only be for a week or two – just until you're well again." *And until I find Benjamin*, Dinah added silently.

Mama stared at her with bloodshot, defeated eyes. She looked exhausted. "Do as you wish, child," she sighed, lying back down again. "I need to sleep."

Dinah's heart was pounding as she stood up. She'd kiss Ollie goodbye and then she'd go to the factories. The idea filled her with terror, but nothing frightened her more than the possibility of never seeing Benjamin again.

THE MATCH FACTORY loomed above Dinah, much of its bulk rising beyond the light of the lonely streetlamp that stood on the corner. Its pale-yellow glow could not illuminate the frame of the building; Dinah only knew it was a match factory at all by the smell, a chemical reek of sulfur and phosphorous that had often clung to Pearl's clothes after a day's work, and by the sign over the door. She'd seen the words there in many advertisements for matches in the newspapers, although she wasn't sure what the words sounded like. *Bryant & May*.

Trembling, Dinah thought of Pearl's dire stories about the girls who spent too much time dipping great frames of matches – four thousand matches in each frame – in the great vats of chemicals, breathing in the heated fumes of white phosphorous. It would start just like a toothache, Pearl had said, until the gums began to swell, and the teeth began to fall out. Later would come an awful smell, a stench like death. And then the very flesh and bone of the jaw would begin to rot.

Dinah took a step back against the crush of muffled men and women hurrying into the factory. She didn't think she was brave enough for this. In her terror, her thoughts reached to a familiar place of safety: Benjamin. His face swam into her consciousness, his dazzling smile, his green eyes. Dinah clenched her jaw. If there was even a chance of finding Benjamin, she had to take it.

Summoning her courage, Dinah fell into step with the mob of faceless workers heading into the factory. They thinned to a trickle by the door, nodding their heads one by one to the overseer who stood just inside the factory. Dinah could hardly believe it was daytime at all – it would be hours before the sun rose. Or perhaps it never rose in this place, she thought, peering past the rows of people heading into the factory ahead of her to stare at its interior. There was a deep red glow coming from somewhere, and it smelled terrible, and there was machinery clanking in a hollow, hungry way. Dinah realized that most of the people in front of her were shorter than she was, because most of them were little girls even younger than Dinah.

She reached the door to find it guarded by an overseer with a long, greasy mustache and twitchy little eyes. He glanced at her, then away, then back at her. "You're not one of our girls," he ground out.

Something about the way he said *girls* made Dinah shudder slightly. "No, sir," she said. "I'm looking for work."

THE SHAMED LITTLE MATCH GIRL

"All of London is looking for work," grumbled the overseer.

Dinah glanced through the crowd of girls heading into the factory. None of them looked like Pearl. She realized that the overseer was saying something. "I'm sorry," she said. "What was that?"

"I said, what experience do you have?" demanded the overseer.

"I... I..." Dinah began to tremble. "N-none, sir. But I can work hard and I'm healthy."

"Ha. Healthy. Not for long," mumbled the little man. He sighed. "Well, turns out that you're lucky. One of the girls died from phossy jaw last week. You can have her place at the dipping vat."

Dinah felt herself go very cold. Suddenly, it was very tempting to turn around and run all the way back to Whitechapel through the dark streets, to climb onto the sleeping pallet and pull the blanket over her head and wait for the world to become less terrifying. Then she remembered that just before they were evicted, Benjamin told her that one of Pearl's friends had died.

This could be the same factory. Maybe she'd even be working at the same vat as Pearl. She clenched her fists. "Please, sir," she said, "I need the work."

"Good." The overseer nodded. "Hey, Aimee."

A girl a little older than Dinah detached herself from the crowd. She gave Dinah an incurious look. "Yes, sir?"

"This is the new girl. Take her to the vat. Show her what to do, and be quick about it," said the overseer. He gave Dinah a last glance. "You'll be paid on Saturday."

Dinah let out a small breath as Aimee led her away. She was trembling from head to toe with terror, but at least she now had two things that she hadn't had when she'd woken that morning: the prospect of making a living, and a tiny kernel of hope.

CHAPTER 4

DINAH'S ARMS ached and trembled with effort. Even after two weeks, the great frames full of matches never felt any lighter, and her muscles cramped in protest as she lowered the frame toward the noxious mixture in the great, bubbling vat. She held her breath as the ends of the long matchsticks plunged into the reeking chemicals, trying to save her lungs from the worst of the fumes that felt like they were burning all the way down.

Straightening slowly, her muscles burning, Dinah lifted the frame and paused for a minute to catch her breath. She was aware that her body was trembling with the effort. Her eyes scanned over the four other girls sharing the vat with her. Aimee was one of them; she hardly spoke, but she stood at Dinah's elbow, and she hadn't spoken a harsh word to her in the past two weeks. Two of the girls standing across from Aimee were sisters who cursed anytime their mouths opened and seemed tougher and more intimidating than most boys on the street.

Then there was the new girl. She'd joined them two days ago, and she hadn't spoken a word. Her eyes remained fixed on her work; her thin arms trembled when she lifted the frame of matches from the vat.

Dinah sidled a step closer to her, tugging the frame along with her. "Hello," she whispered.

The new girl shot her a terrified glance, then looked across the factory floor. It was dotted with similar vats, and in the far corner, the overseer was leaning against the wall. His sharp eyes flitted across all of the girls. Dinah knew that talking with the other girls could cost her a heavy fine from her wages.

"It's all right," she whispered. "He can't hear." She could only hope it was true.

The girl lowered her eyes again and nodded. "Hello," she breathed.

"I need to ask you something," Dinah whispered.

The girl nodded faintly, turning her frame over to plunge the other ends of the matches – two matchsticks were linked together at the start – into the chemical mixture.

"Do you know anyone with the last name Morris?" Dinah asked softly. "Pearl or Benjamin, maybe?"

The girl stared up at her. "I... I don't think so," she whispered.

"You see, I have to find them," said Dinah urgently, keeping her voice low. "They were my friends and they got evicted. I miss them so much, and..."

"Oi." thundered the overseer's voice, right behind her. "You."

Dinah froze. The new girl ducked her head at once, hastily pulling her matches out of the mixture. Dinah didn't have to look around to know that the overseer was marching toward her, his mustache swinging with each movement.

"You, girl." he snapped. "Are you talking?"

Dinah turned her head, keeping her eyes on the floor. "Yes, sir," she admitted. She'd made the mistake of saying no once before; the overseer had ended up punishing the two sisters instead, and they'd hated her ever since.

She didn't see the slap coming until it rang across her face, leaving a trail of fiery pain in its wake. Dinah nearly dropped the matches. She only just managed to maintain her grip on them, her head spinning with the force of the blow.

"That will teach you to flaunt the factory's rules," hissed the overseer. He spat at Dinah's feet and peered over the vat with a hopeful expression, checking that she hadn't dropped any matches; if she had, she knew she'd be in for another slap – and a fine. "No wages for you today," the man added, casually, as if a day's wages meant nothing very much.

"Sir," cried Dinah, appalled.

"Hold your tongue, waif," the overseer barked. "Or do you want me to take an entire week's wages?"

Dinah shook her head, fighting back the tears welling up behind her eyes. The pittance that the match factory paid her was just enough to keep them in bread and rent. If she missed a day's wages, Ollie and Mama would miss a day's food. At least, she was given some weak tea and a dry rusk at lunchtimes in the factory.

"Good," growled the overseer. "Now get back to work."

Dinah lowered her head, tears trickling down her cheeks and into the stinking mass of chemicals. *Oh, Benjamin,* she thought, despair overwhelming her. *Where are you?*

※

BY THE TIME Dinah finally stepped out of the match factory around ten o' clock that night, the bruise on her cheek had turned swollen and throbbing. The cool kiss of snowflakes swirling against it was vaguely soothing; the icy wind, seeking every crack in her threadbare clothing, was not soothing at all. It drove Dinah to walk toward home as fast as she could, even though she felt like her feet would simply wear out and drop off from exhaustion. She'd been standing all day. Her shift at the factory had begun at six o' clock that morning.

Shuffling along amid the tide of people heading home to the slums after a day in the factory, Dinah was barely able to keep her eyes open. She did it anyway, scanning through the streets in search of a familiar face. All of her longed for Benjamin to appear out of the crowds, to light up her entire being with his smile, to run to her and talk to her and make her laugh. Yet the part that actually believed this could happen was growing steadily smaller and smaller.

She dragged herself at last up the rickety staircase to their tenement. At least it was Saturday; she'd just been paid, and even with the loss of some of her wages, she would be able to go to the market tomorrow for a few scraps of food. She thought there might still be a crust of bread or two left for supper tonight, if Mama and Ollie hadn't eaten it all.

"Mama, Ollie!" Dinah tried to sound cheerful as she pushed the door open. "I'm home – Ollie, what on earth is the matter?"

This cry came in response to Ollie, who had rushed across the tenement floor and thrown his little arms around Dinah's waist. He clung to her, his small body shaking from head to foot, his curls pressed tightly against her skirt.

"Ollie, my love, please." Dinah tried to crush the fear that rose up in her. "Tell me what's wrong."

"Mama went," said Ollie.

Something about the way he said those two words made Dinah's blood run cold. "What do you mean, she went?" She crouched down, seizing Ollie's skinny shoulders and searching his brown eyes. "Ollie, what are you talking about?"

Ollie's eyes were red, like he'd spent the day crying.

"She went to work," he said. "She left this morning. She said I should just wait quietly here for you. But Mr. Redstone next door was shouting all day and it was so dark." A fresh burst of tears ran down his grubby cheeks. "I was so alone."

"Oh, Ollie." Dinah wrapped him in her arms, gathering him close to her chest. "I'm so sorry, darling. Don't worry. I'm home now."

Ollie sobbed into her chest, and Dinah bit her lip, squeezing her eyes shut to hold back her own tears. Mama had gone back to work. She told herself that she should be happy, yet a crushing fear continued to press down on her at the thought. She should be joyful to be able to spend her days with Ollie instead of laboring in the match factory. Mama would come home soon with enough money to buy beets and carrots and tripe again, and she could be with Ollie, and she wouldn't get phossy jaw.

If Mama ever came home.

The thought made her swallow hard. Something was telling her that she would be better off keeping her job at the factory.

PART II

CHAPTER 5

Two Years Later

DINAH CROUCHED DOWN by the sleeping pallet, studying Ollie's little face in the pale glow from the low fire burning in the belly of the stove. His cheeks were so hollow, so pale; his curls looked flat and lifeless where they lay across his brow. She sighed softly to herself, sitting back for a moment to just drink in her little brother. Ollie was all she had left. If it wasn't for him, she wasn't sure she would have the courage to ever leave the tenement.

There were only two moments of her day that were truly precious to her. Falling asleep at night with her arms tightly around her little brother, and this moment right before she woke him in the mornings. He always slept so peacefully, his breathing so deep and steady. It was the one moment when Ollie didn't look afraid or lost or simply desperate. He just looked like a little boy at rest, and Dinah wished she could always keep that peace on his face.

But she couldn't. Her shift at the match factory would be starting soon. She reached for his shoulder, touching him gently. "Ollie, darling. It's time to wake up."

His eyelids fluttered. "Mama?" he whispered.

Dinah felt her heart crack, the way it did every time he called her "mama" when he was feverish or dreaming or just waking up. "No, love," she said. "Mama's been gone these two years, remember? It's me, Dinah."

Ollie's eyes opened, and he gazed up at her. His eyes were soft; Dinah searched for disappointment in them and failed to find it. "Are you going away now?" he murmured, his voice thick with sleep.

"Just to work." Dinah brushed a curl out of his eyes. "I'll be back tonight like always. There's still some bread in the box for you, and a little of that sausage for dinner if you want it."

"Thank you," Ollie mumbled, his eyes already closing again.

Dinah bent down to kiss his forehead. "I love you."

"Love you," Ollie said.

She left him slumbering on the sleeping pallet and turned her steps down the hall. Little had changed in the tenement building in the past two years; the drunkard still rented the room where the Morrises had lived. Dinah could hear him snoring away another night of cheap ale behind the grubby curtain; rats had chewed a few new holes in it. She paused by the curtain, feeling tears sting the backs of her eyes. The pain of Benjamin's leaving was still as harsh and fresh as if it had been only yesterday that she watched him walk away. Part of her still believed, every time she saw the curtain move, that Benjamin was about to appear from behind it.

THE SHAMED LITTLE MATCH GIRL

But he never did. And she had never found Pearl at the match factory. It was getting harder and harder to drag herself down those stairs and out into those streets every day, to face the hollow eyes of her coworkers, many of them wearing scarves to hide the face where the very flesh was rotting from their bones.

Mama had never come home. Dinah had tried to grieve for Mama as a person, but it had been hard to find the space for that in her heart amid her worry over how she was going to care for Ollie. Her instinct to keep working at the factory in Mama's absence had proven to be a good one, even though she often came home to Ollie in miserable tears. The money was just enough to pay the rent and more or less feed them.

She stepped out into another gray winter's day. The slum had grown more crowded than ever; she picked her way through the mud that served as a street, avoiding the gazes of the men who huddled in little shelters made of rags and sticks. Excrement lay in the puddles of slush that were everywhere. Her feet squelched in the mud; she felt a cold patch growing on her big toe where her shoe was broken, and the filth began to soak her skin.

She hadn't told Ollie that the rent had gone up. She didn't know why; nor did she know how she was going to pay it come Monday, without letting them both starve.

She looked up at the gray sky, tight and ominous with snow. There was just so much that she didn't know.

***

THE SNOW that the sky had promised that morning was lying thick on the streets that night when Dinah and the rest of the match girls trailed out of the factory, exhausted beyond expression, their feet aching with a familiar dull pain. At their short lunch break, Dinah had seen the snow glittering in a rare burst of sunshine. Now, the night was blacker than black. The snow looked yellow and dirty in the grubby light of the streetlamp.

She felt the reassuring weight of her wages clinking against her thigh with each step where they rested in the pocket of her tattered skirt. It was good to have money, yet she was acutely aware of how pitiful the sum was compared to the week's rent – and the week's food. She forced herself to take deep breaths. Maybe she would find some kind baker who would sell her stale bread at a low price. She would just have to find a way to make it work.

Beside her, Aimee was walking in a similar dull silence. Dinah shot her a sideways look. The older girl was one of few match girls who had survived the past two years; they had become something like friends more out of desperation than anything else. Aimee's eyes had a familiar staring look to them, lined with exhaustion and shot through with redness. But at least the curve of her jawline was pure and clean, with no sign of the swelling that claimed so many lives.

"My rent's gotten more expensive," Dinah said.

Aimee gave her a blear-eyed look. "I'm sorry."

"It's hard. I don't know how I'm going to feed Ollie this week," Dinah admitted. "Maybe it would be easier to sleep on the streets. But..." She shuddered, both at the cold wind that sliced through her thin clothes, and also at the expression in the eyes of a homeless drunkard lying in the doorway of an abandoned factory as they passed. She could feel his eyes slide over her, sparing no part of her body from their penetrating gaze.

"I'm grateful for the old widow whose basement I sleep in," said Aimee. "She's deaf as a post but at least I don't pay rent. She just asks me to carry things and sweep her house sometimes."

"I wish we could find something like that," sighed Dinah.

Aimee shook her head. "Sometimes I don't understand the unfairness of it all," she said. "Why do we have to struggle to find somewhere to sleep and a few scraps to eat, while rich people have more rooms in their houses than they could ever need, and more food on the table than they could ever eat?"

"I don't know," said Dinah.

"They feed their horses better than we're fed," sighed Aimee.

The word *horses* made Dinah think immediately of Benjamin. She thought of his dream of having stables of his own one day, and a sweet pang of longing rose in her heart. She prayed silently that he, at least, had everything he'd ever dreamed of; or at least that he was safe somewhere, and warm, and had a full belly.

The thought of him hurt, like having a dagger plunged into her. But it also gave her just enough hope to force a smile for Aimee.

"Things will get better for us someday," she said, even though she wasn't sure she believed it.

Aimee just sighed. And her sigh said it all.

DINAH STIFLED a yawn as she reached the front door of the tenement building. Sparing a moment to glance up at the building as she reached for the door – it had no handle;

opening it when it was damp was nearly impossible, and so it was kept propped open with a piece of newspaper – she let her eyes run over the fading brickwork and the chipped mortar. She was keenly aware of the men on the street staring on her, and their eyes made her movements hurried. She pulled the door open and slammed it behind her, sealing herself in musty darkness.

Heart hammering, she leaned against the wall for a moment, catching her breath. That was when she heard it: weeping. The desolate sound filtered easily through the thin walls and empty hallways of the tenement building, and it made Dinah's heart freeze.

It was Ollie.

"Ollie?" Dinah didn't care who she woke at this hour. She just started running, pounding up the wooden staircase, heedless of the way it swayed and crackled under her feet. "Ollie."

She reached the top floor at last. Their drunkard neighbor had fallen asleep a few yards short of his door; he didn't stir as Dinah jumped over him, ignoring the loud snores emitting from his open mouth. The sobbing was quieter now, but Dinah could still hear Ollie's efforts to swallow his tears when she reached their door.

"Ollie," she cried again, pushing the door open. It swung around wildly on his single hinge, smacking into the wall. Ollie was a little bundle on his sleeping pallet, barely illuminated by the coal burning in the stove. His knees were drawn up to his chest, and his forehead was pressed to them as he sobbed quietly.

"My darling, please, tell me what's wrong." Dinah's blood rushed in her ears. She was acutely aware that there was no money for a doctor if her little brother was sick. She grabbed his hands, prying them away from his knees. "Ollie, talk to me."

Ollie raised his face to hers. It was streaked with tears, and there was an ugly black bruise forming over his cheekbone. The sight of it set something afire in Dinah's soul. She realized she was trembling as she reached up and cupped his cheek in one hand.

"Who did this to you?" she asked. Her voice came out low and hoarse.

"Oh, Dinah, it don't matter," Ollie sobbed, tears sparkling on his cheeks. "They took my money."

"Money?" Dinah had no idea what he was talking about. "What money?"

"The money I saved to pay the rent with." Ollie lowered his head again, propping up his forehead on his knees. His voice came out muffled. "I heard Mr. Scully tell you that the rent was more expensive now," he whimpered. "I got some money and I saved it up, but some big boys came and hit me, and they took it, and…"

"You got some money?" Dinah grabbed his shoulders. "Oliver Shaw, you tell me right now where that money came from."

He looked up at her, his eyes wide. "P-please," he stammered. "Don't be angry."

"I'm already angry," snapped Dinah. "I told you never to leave this tenement without me. Don't you know what could happen to you on those streets?" An awful shudder trickled down her spine. "Look at what's already happened."

"I'm sorry, Di. I'm sorry." Ollie started crying. "I just wanted to help. I knew we needed money and I just wanted to find a way to get some. You looked so worried."

Dinah felt a softening of her heart even though her fear. "Just tell me what you did," she said.

"I didn't do anything wrong. I just begged. It worked a little. The people gave me some money – there on the street corner by the market – but it's no use. The big boys took it."

Dinah wrapped her arms around Ollie and pulled him into her lap, aware that her heart was pounding with terror. She could believe that begging had been a successful venture for her little brother; he was irresistible with his wide eyes and pretty curls. Yet those same qualities would make him a quick target for kidnappers who wanted to force children to beg – or worse – for their own gains.

"Ollie, I'm not angry," she managed, even though she was: angry and petrified. "But you can never go out of this tenement without me again. *Never*, do you hear?"

He nodded into her chest. "Never," he mumbled.

"Promise me," said Dinah.

He nodded again. "I promise."

She let out a breath of relief, holding him as tightly as she could. She couldn't lose Ollie.

It wasn't the first time she realized he was all she had.

CHAPTER 6

Dinah was trembling from head to foot as she waited in the doorway of the tenement. When she had enough money for rent, she almost looked forward to Monday mornings; the factory opened a little later, and Dinah could sleep for a precious extra hour and still be on time for work after paying Scully the rent.

But today was not one of those Mondays, and there had been no extra sleep. The long night of lying awake and worrying had left Dinah feeling faded and worn out. Now, her exhausted body buzzed with terrified energy. She only had three-quarters of the sum that she owed Scully clutched in her hand. A few more coins waited under the sleeping pallet; just enough to buy a few loaves of bread. She couldn't let Ollie go hungry.

She could only hope that she wasn't about to let him go homeless.

She took a deep breath, but it didn't help. For a moment, she eyed the little pile of coins lying by the curtain opposite her.

Their neighbor worked at the docks; somehow, he always had enough money for rent and booze. Maybe it wouldn't hurt to just take one or two of those unattended coins. He wouldn't hear her; she could hear his snores echoing from within the tenement...

Staring at the curtain made her think of Benjamin, and her grip tightened over the money in her palm. *No.* Benjamin would be ashamed of her for even thinking of stealing. She felt a pit of shame open in her belly and had to fight hard to blink back tears.

"Good morning, Miss Shaw."

Dinah looked up. Scully's greeting was worded cheerfully, but it had something dark and insidious in it, something that was reflected in his flat black eyes. He raked her with a reckless glance as he approached. She felt his eyes linger on her hips, on her chest, and she tugged nervously at her skirt. Her dress was old and faded and much too big, but it couldn't hide the new curves that her growing body kept on adding despite her constant hunger.

She didn't return his greeting, just nodded stiffly and held out her hand. Maybe he'd be so busy staring that he wouldn't notice she was a few shillings short when she dropped the money into his palm.

Indeed, Scully's eyes were fixed firmly on Dinah's neckline as he held out his hand. She dropped the rent into it, careful not to touch his sweaty skin. It looked almost slimy in the gray sunlight from the single window that looked out into a bleary winter's day.

"Good girl," purred Scully, flashing her a grin that penetrated her to the bones and never reached his eyes. Then he looked down into his palm, and Dinah saw his expression freeze. It was as if he didn't need to count the money to know that it wasn't enough. He felt it instinctively. Raising a chubby finger, he poked around at the coins on his palm, then looked up at her with a predatory intensity in his eyes.

"Do you take me for a fool, girl?" he growled.

"No, sir," Dinah stammered, her heart hammering so hard she felt its force might knock her clean off her feet.

"Then what is the meaning of this?" Scully spat, holding up the handful of coins. "Can't you see that you haven't paid me enough?"

Dinah was shaking. "I'm s-sorry, s-sir," she stammered. "I'll pay you. I will. I just need one more week, then I'll have the money." She wasn't sure those words were true.

Scully's eyes roved over her again, and Dinah hated the way they touched every nook and cranny of her, how they probed her. She tried not to shudder too visibly.

"One more week, eh?" Scully murmured.

"Yes, sir." Dinah had heard a softening in his voice and her heart turned over with hope. "Please, sir. I'll pay you back. I'll pay you extra. Oh, please, just give me one more week."

Scully folded his arms. "And where are you going to get the money to pay me next week, if you couldn't pay me this week?" he demanded.

Dinah lowered her eyes, trembling. "I'll find it somehow," she said.

"Ha. A likely story." Scully shook his head. "One week, Miss Shaw. My patience is finished with you. If you haven't paid me everything you owe, *and* some interest, I'll have you out on the streets at once."

Dinah knew it was impossible. She fought back her tears, nodding as quickly as she could. "Yes, sir. I understand, sir. I'll have the money."

Scully snorted. "I don't think so," he said, scathingly voicing the doubts that filled Dinah's own heart. "You'll be homeless in a week, girl." He chuckled, then paused, and his dark eyes grew calculating. "Unless…"

"Unless?" Dinah stepped forward, clutching at the straw. "Oh, sir, is there another way?"

His eyes rambled over her again. "Oh, yes," he said, chuckling again in a mirthless way that gave her chills. "There is another way indeed."

Dinah held her breath, half afraid of what he would say. Scully was silent for a long moment before speaking. "A friend of mine needs a little help with something," he said at last. "I think you would do nicely."

Dinah let out a gusting breath of relief. That didn't sound so bad. "Sir, anything," she said. "If I can work for my rent, I will."

"Oh, you certainly will." Scully gave her one of those tooth-baring smiles of his. "You'll definitely have lots of work to do." He chuckled. "Meet me at the front door of the building next Sunday night."

"Yes, sir. I'll be there. Thank you, sir," said Dinah.

Scully was already walking away. Dinah sagged against the door, weak with relief. It seemed that she had finally found a way out, and whatever it was, she was determined to take it.

THE SHAMED LITTLE MATCH GIRL

Even though Dinah didn't trust Scully as far as she could see him, she still stuck close to him that next Sunday night as they walked through the streets of Whitechapel. It was just before eleven o' clock; Dinah had found Scully waiting at the front door of the tenement building when she'd gotten home from her shift at the match factory. She hadn't even been able to go upstairs and see if poor Ollie was all right. He'd simply given her a gruff order to follow him and then strode off into the slum.

Now Dinah hurried after him, feeling the hem of her skirt drag in the mud and slush, then brush icily against her shins. It was less uncomfortable than the stares from the hollow-eyed men in their ragged shelters who watched her pass.

She wanted to ask Scully where they were going, but she was too afraid. Part of her believed he was leading her into danger. But what choice did she have, other than to follow him? There was nowhere else for her to go. She had to find a way to hold on to that tenement.

Around them, the slum began to recede as they moved into the busier part of Whitechapel. Even at this hour, there were people on the streets now; men with shifting eyes, drunken groups of carousers, women with rouged cheeks and eyes made unnaturally huge and dark with belladonna. Dinah recognized that wide-eyed look from the way her mother would look sometimes coming back from what she had called "work". There was little doubt in Dinah's mind now what her mother had been doing. She shuddered in horror and stayed close to Scully as they turned into another street.

Unlike many of Whitechapel's streets, this one was actually paved. Dinah's shoes padded on the cobbles as she looked around at the ramshackle businesses along the sidewalk. One was filled with drunken singing; others were shuttered but seemed to sell secondhand clothing. One was a pawn shop. A fake diamond glowed in its window.

"Here we are," said Scully.

They had reached a sturdy two-story wooden building that was still lit up despite the late hour. There was no sign over the door; the windows seemed brightly lit, and there was little noise coming from within. Dinah felt a beat of hope in her heart. This place didn't seem too bad.

"This is my friend's place," said Scully, glancing at her. He knocked on the door.

It opened halfway, and a sturdy man with solid shoulders gave Scully a menacing look. "We're full," he said. "Come back in an hour."

Before he could close the door, Scully jammed his foot in it. "Wait." he said. "I'm not a customer. I'm a friend of Bill's."

The big man's eyes narrowed. "You are?"

"Yes," said Scully. "And I've brought him another girl." He grabbed Dinah's arm roughly and plucked her into the light. "I think he'll be quite pleased with her."

The big man raked Dinah with an assessing glance. "She'll do," he said. "I'll get Fred."

A few minutes of silence passed. Dinah ached to ask questions, but Scully seemed content to stand silently, picking his teeth. Eventually, the door swung open again, and a weaselly little man stepped outside. He was wearing colorful clothes that seemed pompous and out of place in the frigid surroundings; his cheeks were very red, his eyes too bright as he looked over Dinah.

"Raymond, my good chap," he said, his words slightly slurred. "What have you brought for me this time?"

"Oh, I've got you something special this time, Fred." Scully grabbed Dinah's arm, yanking her closer. "She's a little young, but I think she'll do just fine."

Fred stepped forward and gave Dinah a calculating look. She hated the pressure of Scully's hand on her arm, but she didn't dare to move. "How old is she?" Fred asked, as if Dinah wasn't even there.

"Fifteen," lied Scully.

Dinah was fourteen, but she didn't say anything. Fred nodded. "Well, some men like 'em young," he said. "And a virgin, I suppose?"

"I wouldn't bring you any less," said Scully, affronted.

Dinah gaped at the way the conversation was going. She suddenly had a terrible knowing about this place, about Fred, and about the way Scully was gripping her arm. Fred came right up to her until they were nose to nose, and his breath huffed in her face, sour and fruity. Dinah gagged.

"Hold still," Fred barked, seizing her chin in cold, strong fingers. She froze, allowing him to turn her head this way and that. "You're a grubby little thing, aren't you?" he grumbled. "We'll have to see about that. But you're right, Raymond. She'll do just fine."

"Good," said Scully. He turned to Dinah. "You'll do ten nights a month. Seven to pay your rent, and three for... interest." His gaze slid down her body as he said it, and when it returned to her eyes, the expression in it made Dinah tremble.

"Sir..." she began.

The door swung open behind Fred. A tall man swaggered out, his clothing rumpled, his gait loose with alcohol. He snickered at Fred and wove off down the street. A moment later, a woman followed, and Dinah felt her heart freeze. The woman wore little more than her underwear; a short skirt barely met her stockings, and her corset left little to the imagination. Her hair was mussed, and the bright rouge on her cheeks was smeared.

"Evenin'," she grunted at Fred. "Just getting some fresh air."

"You do that, darling," grinned Fred. "You've earned your keep twice over tonight."

"I'll earn it three times," said the woman.

Dinah had heard enough. She wrenched her arm away from Scully, backing away. "No." she cried.

"What's that? What's gotten into her?" said Fred.

"Stop that!" Scully barked. "You'll do as you're told. Didn't you say you'd help my friend Fred here in exchange for your rent?"

"You didn't tell me what this place was." Dinah gasped. She wrapped her arms around herself. "This is... is... a *brothel*."

Scully stared at her for a moment. For an awful instant, Dinah thought he might scream at her or hit her again. Instead, to her horror, he threw back his head and began to laugh. The humiliating sound echoed around the street.

"A brothel," he cried, slapping his knee with laughter. "You say it as though you expected anything different."

"I... I..." Dinah was speechless.

"You have no right to be squeamish now, child." Scully jabbed a finger in her direction. "Do you want to pay your rent, or don't you?"

"I do. I do," sobbed Dinah. "But not... not like this."

"Why not?" Scully gave a harsh, barking laugh. "Your mama was the best seller in this place. Why, she'd have men queuing out the door for her."

The mention of Mama smote Dinah like a hot coal to the face. She gasped, remembering a day two years ago when she'd been walking home with dear Benjamin in the gently falling snow. *What do you want to do when you're grown up?* She'd had only one clear answer for him then: She wanted to be nothing like her mother.

Even here, even in the midst of this desperation, Dinah knew that was still what she wanted.

She took a step back. "No," she said. "No, I can't do this."

Scully's eyes narrowed, and his teeth bared. A predator on the hunt. "You have no choice," he hissed. "You'll be homeless unless you go in there and do your work."

"Then I'll be homeless," said Dinah, with all the courage she could muster.

Scully let out a roar of rage and lunged toward her. Dinah's courage was spent. She turned on her heel and ran back into the streets of Whitechapel as fast as her limbs would carry her.

※

DESPITE THE THROBBING ache in her exhausted legs, Dinah took the steps up to the top floor of the tenement building two at a time. The church bell had chimed midnight while she was running; she was breathless now, a stitch blazing in her side, but she knew she only had minutes to get Ollie to safety.

"Ollie!" she shouted, pounding up the hall. "Ollie, wake up."

She kicked open the door, dodging as it nearly hit her, swinging wildly on its rusty hinge. The tenement was warmer than outside; she relished the brief blush of heat on her cheeks as she looked around. Ollie was sitting up on the sleeping pallet. His curls were in all directions, his eyes bleary as he stared at her. "Dinah?" he mumbled.

Dinah seized a sack from its place behind the door and started scooping all of their belongings into it – the one loaf of bread that was still left, the few coins from under the pallet, the handful of coal. "Put your shoes on," she said.

"What? Why?" Ollie pushed back his blanket.

"Do it quickly," Dinah barked. "There's no time."

Ollie's eyes were wide as he reached for the battered pair of shoes she'd bought from a woman whose little boy had just died. She tried not to think of the grief in that woman's eyes as Ollie fumbled with his laces. Grabbing the blanket off the pallet, she rolled it up, trying to breathe normally. Any moment now, Scully would be coming up those steps, irate and ready to take what he believed to be his.

"Come *on*, Ollie," she gasped, throwing the sack over her shoulder.

"Where are we going? What's going on?" Ollie cried.

"We're leaving," said Dinah.

"Leaving? Why?" Ollie's eyes filled with tears. "Is it because of my money that was stolen? Di, this is all my fault."

Dinah felt her heart shatter. She put down the sack and paused to cup her little brother's face in both of her hands, staring into his eyes. "Ollie, my love, none of this has ever been your fault," she said, kissing his forehead. She felt a familiar wave of anguish at the injustice of it all, of having a mother who had conceived this little boy in an awful place like the one she'd so narrowly escaped from, who had then left him alone with only Dinah to care for him. "We just need to go," she added. "Now."

Ollie nodded, finishing up his laces, and Dinah swung the bag over her shoulder again. She was horribly aware that it contained everything they owned in all the world. "Come on, love," she said, taking Ollie's hand.

Somehow the hallway was still clear when they stepped out into it. Dinah stared at the curtain across from them one last time. If only Benjamin could appear from behind it. He would be big and strong now; he'd never have let Dinah go to the brothel. But Benjamin was gone. Long gone.

Perhaps it was time for Dinah to accept that.

She felt her heart rip and turned away. "Let's go."

CHAPTER 7

THE NIGHT WAS FREEZING and so, so dark. Dinah had never been outside at this hour; it was after midnight, six hours before her shift was going to start again, and for the first time she found herself looking forward to going to the match factory. At least there it was warm and well-lit, and there was the promise of something meager to eat at lunchtime. Here, there were only darkness and cold.

She held Ollie's hand tightly as she led him aimlessly through the streets, uncertain of where to go. She knew they couldn't stay in the slum. The men out here would do far worse things to her than the brothel ever could. So she kept walking despite the exhaustion that sucked at her every movement, holding onto Ollie with all of her strength. She kept glancing down to make sure that his curly little head was still close by her side.

She couldn't lose him.

She headed toward the factory district instead, her feet taking her in that direction almost automatically. It was strange and empty at this time of night; the factories loomed on either side of them, huge and silent and hungry. Some of the warehouses had been abandoned, Dinah remembered. Perhaps they could find a place to sleep in one of them.

The first abandoned warehouse they tried turned out to be even colder and wetter than outside. All of the windows had been broken; a great chunk of the roof was torn away, revealing the stars. Snow had melted into frigid pools on the floor. With the wind blowing through the holes in the wall where missing bricks left gaps like lost teeth, it was no use.

As they left it behind and walked underneath the ominous shapes of the factories looming around, Dinah's hope and energy were growing very low when she saw something bright twinkle in the night. She hesitated, clutching Ollie's hand in her numb fingers. There it was – a golden flickering. It looked like firelight.

Firelight. At that point, Dinah was too tired to care who could have made that fire; all she could think of was warmth. "Come on, Ollie," she said. "Not much further."

He nodded, exhausted, and trudged alongside her without complaint. She clung to his hand, praying that they would find somewhere to rest before her shift at the match factory. And what would she do with Ollie then? Where would he stay?

She couldn't think about that. Not now. They just had to get through the night first.

The sparkling light and the crackle of flames led them to another abandoned warehouse. This one was in better condition than the first; all of the windowpanes were broken, and one of the doors stood slightly ajar as if its enormous hinges could no longer move, but the roof and walls were intact. The flickering came from one of the windows. Dinah climbed onto a broken barrel to peer through the window, almost cutting her hands on the jagged bits of broken glass, and her heart both rose and sank. A huge bonfire crackled in the middle of the warehouse floor, golden flames leaping high as if in invitation; but the dark figures of five homeless men sprawled in a circle around the fire.

"What is it, Di?" asked Ollie eagerly. "Is it somewhere warm?"

She looked down at his shivering little frame, his pleading eyes with dark circles beneath them. "Yes," she said. "It's going to be toasty in there."

Ollie's eyes lit up. Dinah prayed that they'd find a way to rest inside without the men noticing. She climbed down from the barrel, scooping Ollie into her arms. "Almost there," she murmured into his curls, the bag bumping on her hip where it hung from Ollie's hands. "Almost safe and warm."

The warehouse was by no means safe, but when they'd slipped through the crack of the door, it did at least prove to be warm – very warm, compared to the street, with the warm glow of the fire warming her face like a happy blush. She crept a little closer, holding Ollie very tightly on her hip. The men were all snoring loudly; empty bottles were scattered around them.

Dinah sagged straight to the floor with relief. At last, it seemed, this cruel world had granted them a brief reprieve from its savagery. Without saying a word, she plucked the blanket from their bag, rolled herself and Ollie up into it, and slept with her head pillowed on the hard floor.

THE SHAMED LITTLE MATCH GIRL

"Oi. What's this, then?"

Dinah jerked awake. A pang of pain ran down her neck; her left foot had gone numb, and her hip ached from the pressure on the floor. She blinked for a moment, utterly disoriented, until the loud voice came again.

"Well, it's a girl, isn't it?"

Dinah sat bolt upright. The fire was burning low; outside the warehouse, it was still very dark. But the homeless men were awake. Two still lounged by the fire; two more were on their feet, stretching, leering, scratching themselves as they gaped at Dinah with open mouths full of rotten teeth. And the fifth stood just a few feet away. He was swaying slightly, but his slack-jawed leer and roving eyes showed no weakness.

She scrambled to her feet, grabbing Ollie's hand. "I'm sorry, sir," she said. "We – we're lost." It was the only thing she could think of to say.

One of the men guffawed. "Sir," he howled, slapping his thigh. "She called you sir."

The leering man took a step closer. "Oh, don't you worry about them, little missy." He reached out and ran the back of an index finger over Dinah's cheek, leaving a grubby smear. "I can be quite the gennulman if I want."

Dinah flinched back, tugging Ollie with her. "We'll just be going," she said.

The man's face twisted, his expression as ugly as his balding head and the empty gaps in his mouth. "Now, don't be a spoil sport," he said. "We just want to have a little fun."

Dinah hated the insinuation in his voice. She hesitated, and he lunged forward, a yellowed claw reaching out to grab her.

She wheeled around, snatching up her sack. "Ollie, run!" she cried.

Ollie didn't need to be told twice. He fled, little feet pounding, and Dinah stayed close beside him. Shouts and running feet sounded behind them, but the men were still very drunk. She heard them toppling into one another and cursing, as they reached the factory door and squeezed out of it into the small hours of another frigid winter's morning.

Breathless, they stopped on the next street corner. Ollie shivered; his breath curled in the air as steam. "Are you all right?" Dinah asked.

"Yes," said Ollie. He wrapped the blanket around himself; Dinah was pleased to see he'd had the presence of mind to grab it. "Where will we go now?"

Dinah sighed. "It can't be long before my shift starts," she said. "We'll go to the factory."

"What about me? What will I do?" Ollie asked.

The question made Dinah feel very cold in the pit of her belly. "We'll find somewhere for you to hide," she said. "Don't worry. Let's go."

It was a short walk to the match factory, and on their way, the church bells chimed a quarter to six. By the time they reached the ugly factory where it squatted among its equally miserable fellows, a large crowd of match girls had already gathered by the door.

Dinah clutched Ollie's hand a little tighter. Maybe, in this mob of girls, she actually stood a chance of smuggling him into the factory unnoticed. "Stay very close to me," she whispered. "And be very quiet. Don't hold my hand – hold on to my skirt."

THE SHAMED LITTLE MATCH GIRL

Ollie nodded, wide-eyed, and tucked himself tightly against Dinah. She slipped into the crowd unnoticed between a pair of girls with their faces bound up in rags, their eyes so deeply focused on their own pain and misery that they didn't spare Dinah or the little boy a second glance. Holding her breath, Dinah stayed close to the other girls. Soon she was right behind Aimee. She kept her eyes focused on the older girl's faded bonnet, not daring to look the overseer in the eye. For an awful instant, she could feel him looking at her as she pushed through the doorway. She waited for him to shout at her, to slap her in the face.

But the shout and the impact never came. Somehow, they were inside the factory, and no one had noticed Ollie.

In the confusion of girls splitting off to the various parts of the factory, Dinah turned to Ollie, almost losing him herself in the crush of people. "Do you see that machine?" she hissed, pointing. A huge, looming hulk of metal was lurking in one corner. It was silent now, but Dinah knew that soon, it would rattle into life – operated by little girls younger than she was – and start wrapping matches into bundles.

"Yes," Ollie breathed.

"Go and hide under it," said Dinah. "Don't move. Don't say a word. Don't do anything until I come and fetch you. Do you understand?"

Ollie's eyes were wide and filled with tears, but he nodded.

"Go," Dinah hissed.

She turned and strode toward the vats, jogging to catch up with Aimee, glancing back at the overseer. He was engaged in shouting at a small girl by the door, and he hadn't seen her. She risked a last glance back toward the machine and just spotted Ollie slipping underneath its metal belly. She could only hope that today wouldn't be one of the rare occasions that the machines were cleaned.

Breathing a little easier, Dinah followed Aimee to the vat. The older girl met her eyes and nodded once – the only acknowledgment they were allowed to exchange. Dinah gave another glance back at the door as they both took a frame and started filling them with matches. The overseer was still shouting at the unlucky girl.

She leaned over to Aimee. "Aimee, I need your help," she whispered.

Aimee shot her a wide-eyed glance. There was something guarded in the way she moved, something that gave Dinah a cold chill of doubt. "Help?" she hissed, turning back to her work. "Be quiet, Dinah. You know we're not allowed to talk."

"The overseer won't hear," said Dinah desperately, hoping it was true. "Please, Aimee. I... I have no one else to ask." *No Mama. No Benjamin. No Aggie.* She felt her eyes fill with tears and tried to blink them back, but one escaped and ran a hot little course down her cheek.

Aimee gave her another wary look. "What is it?" she asked.

"We've been evicted." Dinah sniffed, wiping at her eyes. "My landlord... he wanted me to work in a brothel, and I wouldn't. And now we have nowhere to go."

"You should have gone to the brothel," grumbled Aimee, picking up the match frame and waddling over to the vat, struggling to hold up its weight.

"I couldn't. I just couldn't. What would happen to Ollie?" Dinah followed her, grunting as she lifted her own frame. "Aimee, please, I'm begging you. We have to find somewhere to sleep. We were nearly killed by a gang of homeless men last night." She bent over the vat, feeling the familiar sting as the chemicals seeped into her lungs. "Please, take us to the basement with you."

"The basement?" Aimee shot her another look. "Are you mad? The widow will throw me out."

"Only if she finds out," said Dinah desperately. "Oh, please, please, Aimee. We'll be totally quiet. We'll hide very carefully. Ollie is good at hiding. And – and I'll buy you bread."

"I should never have told you where I sleep," Aimee hissed.

"But you did. And now I'm pleading with you. I'll pay you rent," said Dinah. "I'll pay you anything."

Aimee sighed, turning her face away as she lowered the matches into the deadly mixture that was even now filling their lungs. Dinah glanced up. The overseer was heading toward them, a suspicious look in his eyes as he glared at Dinah. Their brief window of opportunity was rapidly closing.

She blinked back tears, half worried about what would happen if they fell into the phosphorus. Arms cramping, she lowered her own matches toward the awful mixture.

"Fine," Aimee whispered. "I'll do it."

Dinah stared over at her. "You will?"

Aimee nodded once, curtly, and Dinah fell gratefully silent. Seeing that the talking had ceased, the overseer turned and mercifully went the other way.

When Dinah retrieved Ollie from under the match-packaging machine that night, he had been asleep for some time, his head pillowed on his arm, his entire body smeared with the nameless grime that covered every surface of the factory. He coughed quietly as she dragged him out from under the machine.

"Shhh," hissed Aimee, her eyes wide as she glanced around.

"Grab my skirt again," whispered Dinah. "And please, Ollie, don't cough. Hold your breath if you have to." She knew that he'd been breathing in red phosphorus all day and felt a fresh pang of worry run through her. What if he contracted phossy jaw himself?

Somehow, Ollie managed to keep silent. Aimee placed herself between the little boy and the overseer as the wave of exhausted girls headed for the door. They slipped out of the doorway, and then they were out in the streets and Ollie was coughing and coughing, his eyes and nose running.

Dinah wiped at them with her skirt. "Which way?" she asked, taking his little hand in her own.

Aimee sighed. "To the market first," she said, her voice hard. "You have to hold up your end of the arrangement."

"Of course," said Dinah, feeling a pang of fear. She hoped that the few pennies she had left would be enough to buy fresh bread to soothe Aimee's temper. Holding Ollie's hand, she stayed close to Aimee as they headed out of the factory district, leaving Whitechapel far behind. Aimee was heading for a more upper-class part of London. It wasn't long before they were walking on well-lit streets, with paving stones beneath their feet. Dinah's legs were starting to ache again when they reached the market square.

At ten o' clock at night, the square was very quiet, with most shops long closed. But Dinah could already see it was hugely different from the square where she always used to buy bread with Ollie. Instead of tramps and vagrants on the street, there were cabs picking up young ladies in bright clothes and gentlemen with shining silver pocket-watches. Here, vendors had shop fronts with gas lighting and glass windows; all sorts of wares shone in the displays. There was a milliner's displaying dresses of all colors, a grocer with fresh green vegetables, even a sweet shop with brightly wrapped candies and sweetmeats in the windows. Ollie's eyes lit up at the sight of the sweets.

"Di, look at those." he gasped. "Can I have some?"

"No, darling," said Dinah. "Look – the shop's closed."

"And we're too poor for such nonsense in any case," barked Aimee. "Here – the bakery. It's closed now but if you go around the back, the baker will sell you his stale bread cheaply. Buy as much as you can."

Dinah hesitated. "Me?" she said.

"Yes, you." Aimee grabbed Ollie's arm. "I'll wait here with the boy."

Dinah met Aimee's eyes. The girl's jaw was clenched, and she knew that arguing would be utterly useless. She gave Ollie a forced smile and turned toward the bakery, walking as briskly as she could, keeping her hands in her pockets and clenched around her precious few coins.

The bakery bordered on a narrow alley, and Dinah spotted the back doorway, shadowy against the gloom. She guessed that was where she had to go to find the baker's stale bread. Glancing around, she paused at the entrance of the alley. It seemed mostly empty; the only person she could see was a tall gentleman with steel gray whiskers, who was walking along the sidewalk by the road, heading for a carriage waiting by the corner.

She didn't want to get in the gentleman's way. She knew from experience that rich gentlemen were never to be trusted. Stepping into the alley, she hastened over to the door and knocked once, briskly.

It swung open at once. A sturdy man with great pink fists like two hams gave her a harsh look. "What do you want?" he said.

"Stale bread, sir, if you please." Dinah held out her coins, trembling. "As much as this can buy."

He glanced over them. "Ha. You'll get half a loaf for that."

"Sir, please." Dinah felt a pang of panic. "My little brother is only seven. He's going to starve. Please, help..."

His blow came out of nowhere, a quick, back-handed cuff that struck her on the temple and sent her staggering back against the alley wall. She heard the patter as her coins were flung down at her feet. "Filthy wretch." he barked. "What do you think I care? Get away, or I'll set my dog on you."

Tears poured down Dinah's cheeks. She crouched down, scrambling to pick up the coins.

"Go!" barked the baker, raising another threatening hand.

"If you please, good sir." The voice rose through the alleyway, pure and calm. "Pray, don't raise another hand to the lady, or I shall be very upset."

Dinah looked up. The gentleman with the gray whiskers was coming down the alley, looking out of place with his ivory-

THE SHAMED LITTLE MATCH GIRL

handled walking stick and well-cut, bottle green suit. He gave the baker a severe look and reached for Dinah's arm. His grip was unexpectedly gentle; Dinah allowed herself to be pulled to her feet and was surprised when he let her go as soon as she was standing.

"Mr. Hughes, sir." The baker's attitude changed at once. An ingratiating smile flooded his features, and he hunched his shoulders, rubbing his hands together. "This waif here was trying to steal from me, you see. I..."

"No, Gibson, I don't see," said Mr. Hughes icily. "I know that this young lady was simply trying to buy some bread from you. Why, can't you see that the poor creature is on the brink of starvation?" He tapped his stick twice on the ground, briskly. "Be a good fellow and bring three of your freshest loaves at once."

The baker paused. "Sir..."

"At once, Gibson," ordered Mr. Hughes, "or I'm afraid my good friend at the *Weekly Dispatch* will hear what I have to say about the way you treat customers at this establishment."

The baker's eyes widened. "Yes, sir. Right away, sir," he said, and disappeared into the bakery.

Dinah stepped back, feeling suddenly very trapped in this dark alley with the gentleman. To her surprise, Mr. Hughes didn't come any closer. He gave her a brief smile. "Are you hurt, young lady?"

"N-not at all, sir," said Dinah. "Thank you, sir." She backed away a little more.

"I assume you have every right to be frightened." Mr. Hughes sighed. "Where do you live?"

"Close by, sir," said Dinah quickly. She didn't want him to think that she was homeless.

"I see." Mr. Hughes nodded.

The door swung open again, and the baker held out three fresh loaves in their paper bags. "Take 'em," he barked.

Dinah grabbed them, bewildered and delighted by the warm weight of them. "Oh, thank you, sir."

"Goodbye," said the baker, and slammed the door.

Mr. Hughes doffed his hat to her as if she was a lady. "Good evening to you, Miss...?"

"Shaw," said Dinah nervously. "Dinah Shaw."

"Good evening to you, Miss Shaw," said Mr. Hughes. "I hope to have the pleasure of your company another time."

Those words made every part of Dinah's body spring tight with fear, but Mr. Hughes simply turned and walked out of the alley. The moment he was gone, Dinah broke into a dead run. And she didn't slow down until she had pressed the loaves of bread into Aimee's arms.

CHAPTER 8

Dinah could taste the first hints of spring in the night air as she walked. Her shoulders were hunched, her hands tucked deeply into the pockets of her coat. Aimee kept pace with her, but they didn't speak. They hadn't really spoken in months, even though they now lived together.

Perhaps *because* they now lived together. Dinah shot a sideways glance at Aimee, trying to judge the older girl's mood. Aimee's mouth was pressed into a hard, bitter line. Dinah hurriedly lowered her eyes to the filthy sidewalk again. She knew she'd made an awful mistake by dropping a match on the ground while she was filling her frame at the factory. Of course, her punishment had been the loss of the day's wages, and that meant less food for everyone—and anger from Aimee.

She couldn't afford to make Aimee angry. Dinah swallowed hard, trying not to think of what would happen to them if Aimee decided to throw them out of the basement. She felt a pair of eyes drilling into her and glanced up briefly to see a scruffy street boy lounging on some broken boxes in a nearby alley. As they passed, he held up a half-drunk bottle of something and let out a wolf whistle.

Dinah's cheeks burned with shame. She quickened her step, feeling his eyes follow her.

"Slow down," snapped Aimee. "Don't you know my legs are tired?"

"Yes, Aimee," said Dinah quickly, obediently slowing her pace. She hated the fact that she could feel the boy's eyes dwelling on her growing curves.

"You could make good money like that, you know," said Aimee.

Dinah glanced at her. "Like what?"

Aimee shrugged. "You know. Doing what your mother did."

Dinah lowered her eyes again, ashamed that she, too, had considered that fact. So many times over the last few months, when she and Ollie were shivering on the cold floor of the basement or she was enduring yet another tongue-lashing from Aimee, she'd wondered if it wouldn't have been better to go along with what Scully and Fred wanted. But each time she thought about it, she felt her stomach turn.

They'd reached the crossroads near the market square, and Aimee stopped abruptly, digging in her pocket for a few pennies. "Here. Get food," she ordered. "And make it quick. I'm hungry."

"Yes, Aimee," said Dinah, taking the money.

"I'll be at home." Aimee turned and stalked away.

Dinah felt a weight lift from her shoulders as soon as Aimee was gone. She walked briskly toward the bakery, flexing her stiff neck this way and that. The overseer had given her a stunning blow with his club when she'd dropped the match, and something had hurt her neck in the fall.

When she neared the bakery, she wasn't surprised to see Mr. Hughes standing by the corner, leaning on his walking stick. He was wearing a plum suit this evening with a top hat that had a green ribbon around it, and he gave her a gentle smile as she approached. "Good evening, Miss Shaw."

Dinah kept her distance from him more out of habit than anything else; there was no real fear in her as she approached the bakery. "Hello, sir," she said politely.

"How was your work today?" asked Mr. Hughes.

"Oh, it was awful." Dinah paused a safe distance from him and dredged up a smile. "I dropped a match, and they took away my day's wage."

"For dropping a single match?" cried Mr. Hughes, his eyes widening with real concern.

"Yes, that's how it goes, sir," said Dinah. "If you please, sir, I'm very hungry. I would like to buy some bread before the baker closes."

"It's too late for that, I'm afraid, but don't you worry." Mr. Hughes picked up a paper bag that had been leaning against the bakery wall beside him. "Two dozen of his finest white rolls, freshly baked."

Dinah let out an involuntary gasp at the delightful smell of them. Forgetting her caution for a moment, she stepped forward, almost snatching the bag from Mr. Hughes' hands. "Oh, sir." she cried, pulling out one of the rolls. Its smell was absolutely delicious. She couldn't resist taking just one bite, and its sweet, wholesome flavor filled her mouth.

"I know you and your friend and brother must be very hungry," said Mr. Hughes gently. "Now, I'm going to be in the country for a few days for business, Miss Shaw, but I don't want you to have any difficulty with food." He dug in his pocket and produced a bright, shiny pound – more money than Dinah had ever held in her hand in all her life. "Hide it quickly," he urged, glancing around. "I don't want you to be pickpocketed."

Dinah felt that old wariness rise in her. She backed away a few steps. "Sir... I don't..." She met his eyes. "I can't repay you," she said flatly.

She expected his gaze to slip downwards, over her chest, her hips, but his eyes held hers. "I don't expect you to, Miss Shaw," he said. "Good day."

He gently tossed the shiny pound at her feet, lifted his hat and strode off. The moment his back was turned, Dinah snatched the pound up into her hands, letting out a breath of relief. She paused for a moment to watch Mr. Hughes' coat-tails waft in the breeze as he walked away, digging his stick into the ground with every stride.

He was a puzzle that she still couldn't solve. His gaze was so kind, and yet she could never shake the feeling that there was something he wanted from her.

***

THE RICH WIDOW lived on one of the prettiest streets Dinah had ever seen. She didn't know if the rest of London was anything like this, but to her, this was the loveliest place in all the world. She slowed her steps as she turned into the street. This was the one moment of beauty she had in her day, and she cherished it dearly.

The houses here didn't have the sheer scale or the sweeping grandeur of the manor houses – she had seen a few woodcuts of them in the newspapers – but they all had a sturdy look about them, and all were bigger than the entire tenement building where she had stayed with Ollie and Mama. Their walls were all freshly painted, many of them a cheery white; there were lace curtains in all of the windows. Now, with the worst edge of winter fading from the air, many of the houses sported window boxes and little strips of garden in the front. Nothing yet bloomed, except a snowdrop here and there, but the bright green of the plants reminded her so much of Benjamin's eyes.

Oh, Benjamin. Dinah reached into her pocket and folded her fingers around the heavy pound coin. She hoped with all of her heart that he was safe somewhere.

Before she reached the widow's home, Dinah ducked into a narrow alley between two of the houses. There were no drunkards or broken bottles here, just an empty space where people put their bins, but at least no one noticed her as she slipped behind the houses. She reached the widow's house in a few moments, and Aimee pushed the door of the basement open.

"You're here," she said. "Did you bring food?"

Dinah met her eyes, feeling the warmth of the fresh bread rolls where she held them tightly. For a moment, she considered telling Aimee about the pound coin, but before she could say anything Ollie appeared behind Aimee. "Oh, please, Di," he said. "I'm so hungry."

"Ollie." Dinah dropped the coin back into her pocket. "What's happened to you?"

Ollie gave her a sullen look. "Nothing. I fell," he said.

She could tell he was lying just by the tone of his voice, and also by the fact that the bruise on his face was spread over his cheekbone. It was ugly, black and purple and red. "Tell me what happened." she ordered.

Tears filled Ollie's eyes. "I just wanted to help," he said.

"How many times have I told you that the best thing you can do is to stay here in the basement?" Dinah cried.

Ollie sank down onto the single, filthy blanket he still shared with Dinah. "I got two oranges," he said.

"How, Ollie?" Dinah asked. "Where?"

"I stole them." Ollie buried his face in his hands and started sobbing. "I stole them, Di. I was hungry. We're all hungry."

"Don't listen to her, Ollie." Aimee sat down with a huff on her sleeping pallet. "What's in the bag?" she demanded of Dinah.

Dinah wasn't hungry anymore. She handed over the paper bag. "Fresh rolls," she muttered. "Ollie, you need to stay in the basement. Anything could happen to you out there. Who hit you?"

"The grocer," mumbled Ollie, but he'd looked up at the sound of the paper bag crinkling.

Aimee tossed him a roll. He caught it, his grubby fingers smearing its white surface, and simply stared at it in awe for a moment before he started tearing into it with ravenous bites. "Don't listen to her," she repeated. "You did well, Ollie. It's useful having you here in the basement."

Dinah gritted her teeth, feeling a wave of helpless fury in rise in her. She knew she couldn't contradict Aimee – not when their lives relied on her allowing them to stay with her. But as happy as it made Aimee when Ollie stole extra food, Dinah couldn't allow it.

She watched him eat, his tears still running down his bruised cheeks, shooting her frightened glances from the corner of his eye. Sighing, she sank down beside him, wrapping an arm around his shoulders. He deserved so much better than all this. He deserved to make something of himself one day. She pictured him in a plum suit and top hat, like Mr. Hughes, and it made her smile.

She had to find a way for Ollie to have a better life, and he couldn't do it without an education.

She reached into her pocket and wrapped her hand around the pound coin. Maybe she'd just found a way to give him one.

SPRING WAS COMING, but there was still a painful chill in the air at ten to six the next morning. It made Dinah's fingers ache constantly. She stood in front of the silent factory, blowing on them, her eyes scanning the crowd of match girls surrounding them.

Even though the factory's doors only opened at six o' clock sharp, all of the girls knew better than to be even one minute late. Despite their fourteen-hour shifts, a few minutes of tardiness could cost them an entire day's wage. No one could risk that. Dinah knew as well as everyone that the pitiful salary of a match girl was barely enough for a few morsels of food at the end of the day.

Her eyes lit on a girl about her own age, with tired eyes and red curls. Checking to make sure that Aimee was still busy talking with some of her new friends – Dinah's status as a friend seemed to have vanished the moment they'd moved into the basement – she hurried over to the girl.

"Hello, Ginger," she said softly.

Ginger raised mournful eyes that were a blue so pale they looked almost translucent, as if the color had been washed out of them with crying. "Di," she said.

It had become a habit for Dinah to run her eyes over the curve of each girl's face, a morbid fear always gathering in the pit of her belly. Was that a lump developing at the corner of Ginger's jaw? Dinah didn't want to look or think about it. Instead, she forced a smile. "How are you today?"

Ginger stared at her with those hollow eyes. "I'm alive," she said.

Alive. Dinah realized grimly that that was the best any of the match girls could hope for. She felt determination rise in her belly. She couldn't let that become Ollie's fate, too. "Ginger," she said, delicately, "does your brother still remember how to read?"

Ginger's eyes flickered. "Yes," she said. "Of course. George had a tutor in the old days, before Papa died and left Mama in more debt than the family could ever pay." She let out a wispy little sigh that seemed empty somehow, as if all her sorrow had been spent.

"Well, maybe I can help you," said Dinah, "if George can help me."

Wariness filled Ginger's eyes. "What are you talking about?"

Dinah glanced around. No one was watching, so she reached into her pocket and pulled out the pound just long enough that a glint of light from the streetlamp could ripple over its surface. Ginger's eyes grew huge and round and animated. "Dinah," she gasped.

"It's yours," said Dinah, "if George will come to the basement every day and teach Ollie how to read. I'll pay you more, in a few months. This is just to start." She didn't know where more money would come from, and her thoughts flashed to Mr. Hughes. Her stomach clenched at the idea of asking the older man for more help. Who knew what he would demand in return? But she had to do this for Ollie.

Ginger held out her hand. "I'll send him tomorrow morning first thing," she said. "I promise."

Dinah slipped the pound into her fingers. "Good."

Even though it felt strange and perhaps even foolish to let go of all that money, a deep relief flooded Dinah's gut the moment Ginger thrust the pound into her pocket and scurried into the factory. She would live this dreadful life a thousand times if she could spare her brother from living it.

CHAPTER 9

THE BACK of Aimee's hand thudded across Dinah's cheekbone with a force that threw her backwards onto the sidewalk. Despite the balmy sun of late spring that was beaming down onto the city, the sidewalk itself felt icy where it met her flesh, as if it held the memory of winter deep within its frozen heart. Taken utterly by surprise, Dinah blinked up at Aimee, breathless and hurt.

"What's going on?" Aimee shouted. "What are you keeping from me, Dinah?"

Dinah raised a hand to the throbbing welt that was rising on her jawline from the blow. "Wh-what do you mean?"

"You know very well what I mean," Aimee spat.

Dinah did. She was still bursting with pride from a moment earlier that morning when Ollie had been quietly gazing down at a scrap of old newspaper while he ate his meager Sunday breakfast. At first, Dinah had thought that he was just looking at the woodcuts, as he often did. Then he held up the page to her and said, "Look, Di. It's about the war in America." Dinah's heart had felt that it might burst with pride.

"Ollie was *reading*," Aimee hissed. "How did he learn that?" Her eyes were furious.

Dinah slowly got to her feet. She'd known that sometime, in his excitement, her brother would let his secret slip. She shot a glance over toward the bakery, where Aimee had sent Ollie to buy some stale bread before confronting Dinah on the street corner. Ollie was still safely inside.

"I... I want him to have a better life," said Dinah. "I want him to have an education."

Aimee's eyes narrowed. "Dinah, you haven't been paying someone to teach him how to read, have you?"

Dinah stared into Aimee's eyes, her heart thundering. She didn't want to anger the girl who'd effectively become their landlady, but she knew there was no lying about this. Her pride overruled her fear. "Yes." she said. "Yes, I have. I've been paying Ginger's brother to teach him. And Ollie is clever, Aimee, he's very, very clever. Look at how he's reading the paper already, and he's only been learning for a few months."

"How could you?" Aimee shrieked. "How could you pay for your brother to have *lessons* when we're on the brink of starving to death?"

"Because I have to give him a better life," said Dinah. "I *have* to, Aimee."

Aimee glared at Dinah for a long, furious moment. Dinah held her breath, praying that Aimee would forgive her. The fact that she'd waited for Ollie to be out of earshot before accusing Dinah gave her hope that perhaps her little brother had penetrated even Aimee's cold heart.

"You're a traitor," Aimee hissed. She spat at Dinah's feet. "I'm going home. Finish the shopping."

Dinah felt her shoulders sag as Aimee turned on her heel and strode away. Aimee hadn't thrown them out of the basement. Compared with that appalling possibility, a blow to the face and a tongue-lashing were nothing.

The bell of the bakery door jingled behind Dinah, and she turned to see Ollie skipping out, clutching a brown paper bag to his chest. "Di. I got a loaf of bread." he called out. "And I even worked out the change that the baker had to give me."

Dinah couldn't help a laugh of delight. "Oh, Ollie, you're so clever," she said.

"Did I do something wrong?" Ollie asked, his eyes widening as they dwelt on her swollen jaw. "I knew I shouldn't have told you about the paper. Di, I'm so sorry." His eyes started to fill with tears.

"Ollie, no." Dinah put a hand on his shoulder. "You did nothing wrong at all."

"But Aimee was angry with you. She hit you again," said Ollie.

"It's all right," said Dinah. "The main thing is, you're learning, and you're doing it really well." She bent to kiss his forehead. "That's all that matters. One day you're going to have a better life because of your education, Ollie. I know it."

Ollie wiped at his tears. "And you will too," he said. "I promise."

Dinah forced a smile. "And me," she said, even though she knew the words likely weren't true. "Come on. Let's go to the grocer's. I'm sure we can get some of those wilted carrots that Aimee likes – then she'll be nicer."

Walking down the market square, Dinah tried to ignore the throbbing of her feet. They never quite seemed to stop aching; those long shifts were brutal on them, and her single day off each week was mostly spent trying to find a place to buy as much food as possible for as little money as possible. At least on Sundays the square was fairly quiet. A few well-to-do couples strolled among the shops, shooting irritated glances at Dinah and Ollie, as if the two ragged children were ruining their pretty square.

The grocer with the wilted carrots, however, ran a grubby little shop on one of the narrow side streets leading off the square. Dinah held Ollie's hand tightly as they turned down the street. It was grimy enough to serve as a reminder that this nice district was still within a short distance of the factories and even of Whitechapel itself. About halfway down the street, just opposite the grocer, Dinah could see three young men lounging about in the mouth of an alley. They were passing a bottle of alcohol around, and already had the roving eyes and loose-lipped leers of men who had spent the day drinking already.

Dinah lowered her eyes, not looking at them, as she hurried toward the grocer's door. Maybe if she didn't look at them, they would pay her no mind. It was, as always, a false hope.

"Good mornin'," one of them called out, his voice a low, drawn-out slur.

Dinah nodded once and kept walking. But one of the young men was already on his feet. He had a shaggy beard and wild eyes, and he wove toward Dinah, his eyes focused and predatory. "Where's your manners, little missy?" he demanded, stopping right in front of the grocer's door.

Dinah stopped sharply, holding Ollie's hand tightly. She could feel it shaking. "Excuse me, sir," she said. "I'm in a hurry." She failed to hide the quaver in her voice; the other two men had also gotten up and were flanking the bearded one.

"Oh, in a hurry, are you?" The bearded man grinned, revealing an awful set of black and yellow teeth. "A fast woman, isn't she?"

A chorus of disgusting chuckles came from the other men. Dinah began to back away, and the bearded man lunged, seizing the front of her dress. She felt his fingers rake over her skin and pulled back with a yelp; her dress sprang tight, yanking her back.

"Now, now, missy," hissed the man, leaning closer, his reeking breath in her face. "Don't spoil our fun."

"Ollie, run!" Dinah screamed. "Run!"

The man whirled her around, slamming her up against the wall of the grocer's shop. "Shut up," he yelled, a thin spray of spittle prickling on her face.

"So young. So soft," murmured one of the other men, leaning closer to where Dinah was writhing and gasping against the wall. He reached out and brushed the back of one forefinger over her cheek. She gasped, pulling her head away, and the man seized her painfully by the chin. "Stop that at once," he snapped.

"Let me go!" Dinah cried, kicking out frantically, but the bearded man had already rammed his body up against hers. He was filthy and sweaty and pressing against her with a force

THE SHAMED LITTLE MATCH GIRL

that made it hard to breathe. His breath was right in her face as he reached for her dress...

Hoofbeats rang on the street. "Unhand her, you foul creatures," cried a high voice, punctuated by the shrill bell of a horse's whinny.

Dinah heard a gasp. Abruptly, the bearded man let go of her, and she fell to the floor with a thump that rattled all of her bones. On her hands and knees, gasping with pain and terror, her world was blurred with tears. She heard shouts, cries of pain, the hammer of hooves, and a sturdy voice raised in righteous anger. Then there were running feet, and silence.

She heard the horseman dismount, and running feet coming toward her. "Are you all right?"

For a moment, the pain and fear and the chaos of it all made Dinah believe that it was Benjamin. She looked up, reaching out in joy and terror, but the face was older and lined and edged with a beard the color of steel.

"Oh," she gasped, sitting back. "Mr. Hughes." She was suddenly very aware of her dress rucked up around her knees, and grasped at it frantically, pulling it down. The front of her dress was slightly torn; she clutched at it, panicking.

Mr. Hughes was pulling off his coat – it was navy blue this time – and holding it out to her. "My dearest Miss Shaw, did they hurt you?" he asked, his eyes flashing with a passion she hadn't known in him before.

"N-no. They wanted to. But they didn't." Dinah gratefully grabbed his coat and pulled it around her shoulders. He stepped back, and she got to her feet, feeling safer and more decent with the sturdy fabric covering her. Still, her legs felt wobbly and disjointed; she wavered, and Mr. Hughes stepped forward to grasp her gently by the elbows, keeping her at arm's length. She felt a wave of gratitude as she found her feet; as soon as she felt steady, he let her go, retreating once again to a respectful distance.

"Dinah," cried a voice from the street. "Di. Di!"

She turned. Ollie came running down the street as fast as he could, tears pouring down his cheeks. "Di," he cried, leaping up to her and throwing his arms around her waist. "Oh, Di, are you all right?"

"I'm just fine, Ollie," said Dinah, wrapping her arms around him in trembling gratitude. "I'm fine."

She looked up. Mr. Hughes was watching her. His eyes were so gentle, yet there was something else in them. It was nothing like the predatory hunger that she'd seen in the eyes of the bearded man who had run away; it was more of a quiet longing. But it still worried her.

She pushed the thought away quickly as she clutched his coat close around her shoulders. He'd just saved her from a fate that she had learned to dread more than anything else. "Oh, Mr. Hughes," she said. "I don't know how to thank you."

Mr. Hughes smiled in his shirtsleeves as he doffed his top hat. "I need no thanks for coming to the succor of such a good young lady," he said. "Is your little brother all right?"

"He's fine." Dinah bent to kiss him. "Oh, Ollie, did you call Mr. Hughes?"

"He was riding down the street," said Ollie. He looked up at the older man. "I knew he'd help."

"Of course," said Mr. Hughes. He reached into his pocket for a little candy, wrapped in bright paper, and dropped it into Ollie's hand. Quickly, he added a half-crown. "Now take care of yourself, Miss Shaw," he said, his eyes meeting hers for a vulnerable moment. Then he swung back onto his horse and trotted off down the street.

And Dinah couldn't resist watching him go.

※

The bruise that Aimee had left on Dinah's jaw had gone from purple to a faded yellow, and only stung now if she pressed it. Still, the icy atmosphere simmered between them. As Dinah pulled on Mr. Hughes' coat – he had told her to keep it; she had had to rub a little mud into the fine fabric to keep it from being stolen, but it was wonderfully warm – she shot a glance across the basement at where Aimee was getting ready to leave. The girl's face was as hard and gray as if it had been carved from stone. Dinah was starting to think that her heart, too, was composed of something much colder than flesh these days.

Ollie, still curled up under his blanket, noticed Dinah's eyes dwelling on Aimee. "Why is she angry with you?" he whispered to Dinah.

Dinah knelt to kiss him. "Hush, my love. It's too early for you to be awake. Go back to sleep."

Ollie lay back down, but his eyes were troubled. "I know it's because of me," he said.

"Never." Dinah kissed him again.

"I want to help you, Di." Ollie's eyes filled with tears. "I want you to have a better life, too."

"The best thing you can do for me is to keep on learning to read and being a good boy like you are, Ollie," said Dinah. "That's all I want from this life."

Ollie nodded, his face relaxing a little.

"Be good. I'll see you tonight." Dinah ran a hand through his curls and then hurried to the door, barely catching it as it swung shut behind Aimee.

With the older girl still simmering with rage almost a week later, Dinah realized there was no point in sticking with Aimee on the road to the factory. She would walk alone. At this hour in the morning, the streets, at least, were safer than at night; most of the drunkards were asleep. Dinah shoved her hands into the pockets of Mr. Hughes' coat. Even with summer drawing nearer, the basement was cold, and Dinah looked forward to the walk to warm her up.

Her feet carried her toward the factory mechanically, her eyes unfocused on the sidewalk as she moved from the light of one streetlamp to the other. The nearer she came to the factory district, the more crowded the streets became, even this early in the morning. Like her, most other factory workers started at six o' clock. They were a dull-eyed drove of exhausted human beings, their faces pale and expressionless, stumbling off to another fourteen-hour shift of mind-numbing work. Horses and carts started to bustle up and down in the streets, too. Most of the horses were broken-down old creatures with jutting hip bones and thin necks, as exhausted of life as their masters.

One of them, though, somehow caught Dinah's eye about a block away from the factory district. Its coat flashed in the light of the nearby streetlamp, and Dinah paused, staring. It was trotting along the road with a cab behind it, its hooves clip-clopping in a bright rhythm among the dreary trudge of the morning traffic. It was so strange to see something beautiful and cheerful here that she couldn't resist watching it pass. It was pulling a plain brougham, light and well-cared for, and its coachman sat up as straight as a ramrod. It flashed past her on the street, a groom clinging on to the back of the brougham as it rattled through the traffic. As they neared the street corner, the groom glanced back.

And his eyes were green. Forest green.

"Benjamin!" The word tore from Dinah's throat before she could stop it. A wild hope sprang in her heart even as the brougham disappeared among the crush of traffic. She knew it was foolish, she knew it was impossible – but she couldn't help herself. She broke into a run, shoving others aside, dashing recklessly into the street. Voices shouted, hooves slammed in panic, and Dinah didn't care. The brougham reappeared for a moment among the chaos, turning down a side street, and she redoubled her pace when she saw the few wisps of red curls under the groom's hat.

When she pounded over the corner, pushing past a newspaper vendor and sending his pages blowing in the morning breeze, the brougham had somehow, miraculously, come to a halt. It was standing at the office door of one of the factories; the coachman had already opened the door, and a gentleman in a black tailcoat was stepping out. Of the groom, there was no sign.

Dinah was suddenly aware of the trail of shouts and discontentment she had left behind her, and an overwhelming nervousness struck her. She slowed down and stopped beneath a streetlamp, her heart hammering, gasping for breath.

She must have imagined it. Somewhere in her exhausted, addled brain, she had imagined Benjamin clinging to the back of that brougham.

The coachman closed the door as the gentleman disappeared into the office. "I'm goin' to have a smoke," he announced. "Watch the hoss, boy."

"Yes, sir," said a calm, clear voice that lanced into Dinah's heart like a beam of warming sunlight. The coachman strode away, and Benjamin stepped out from behind the horse, a nosebag in one hand, a stable rubber in the other.

This time, Dinah didn't seem to have enough air in her lungs to cry out. She couldn't breathe or run forward or move a single muscle or do anything except stand staring at him. He was older now; he would be sixteen or seventeen, Dinah remembered, and there was a scattering of stubble on the smooth line of his jaw. But the smile he gave the horse was still the same, and his eyes…

They still reminded Dinah of that tree on the corner of the Whitechapel slum.

He hooked the nosebag over the horse's ears and patted the animal's neck as it started to champ the contents vigorously. "Good old chap," he said. "What a good chap."

He began to run the stable rubber over the horse's gleaming coat, cleaning away the foamy sweat where the harness had rubbed, and bent to lift each of its legs in turn. Dinah still couldn't move, until he straightened up from lifting a hind foot and looked her directly in the eyes.

He froze, too, but only for an instant. "Dinah?" he breathed.

"Benjamin." The name gushed out of her almost unbidden, and then she was running to him, her arms held out, tears of

THE SHAMED LITTLE MATCH GIRL

joy pouring down her cheeks. She nearly bowled him over, but his strong arms caught her and swept her around in a half circle before setting her lightly back on her feet. She clung to the lapels of his coat, staring up into those glorious green eyes, pressed close against him. She wasn't sure if the thumping she felt was his heart or hers.

"Dinah. Oh, Dinah." He said her name the way a drowning man would gasp for air, his hands still resting on her arms. "It's been so long."

"Four and a half years," said Dinah.

"You've – you've grown," said Benjamin.

Dinah realized she was tipping her head back to look him in the eye. "So have you." she gasped. "And you look so well. And you're working with horses."

"Yes." Benjamin laughed. "I'm working for a livery stable. Mama remarried."

"What?" cried Dinah, both shocked and delighted. She could hardly imagine Aggie even looking at a man again, after what Benjamin's father had done to their family.

"He's a good man. A blacksmith," said Benjamin. "Pearl doesn't have to work for the match factory anymore. She's a seamstress now. They live in a tenement, but it's a good one, with no holes in the walls."

"Benjamin, that is so wonderful." Dinah felt weak at the knees; she clung to him a little, feeling as though some of her prayers had finally been answered. "I'm so glad. I've never stopped thinking about you."

"Nor have I stopped thinking about you," said Benjamin tenderly, his eyes searching hers. "Oh, Di, I've missed you so much. How are you?"

Dinah felt her toes curl inside her broken shoes. How could she tell her sad story to this happy, happy young man whose dreams were all coming true? She couldn't tell him about Scully or Aimee or the basement. She stepped back, dropping her hands to her sides again. "Oh – we're fine," she said. "I've got a job. Ollie's busy learning how to read."

He saw through her at once; she could tell by the pity in his voice. "I'm glad to hear about Ollie," he said gently. "How is your mother?"

Dinah looked up at him. His eyes were so caring, so tender. A wild hope leaped in her. Maybe she had found a way out. Maybe Benjamin would help her, the way he always used to do.

"Benjamin..." she began.

The church bell chimed nearby; a quarter to six. A jolt of fear ran through Dinah. She would be late to work unless she ran right away, and she couldn't afford to lose that job. Besides Mr. Hughes, it was the only thing keeping her and Ollie alive.

"I have to go," she said, staring back up at him.

"Don't worry. It's all right," said Benjamin, stepping forward to rest a hand on her arm. "This gentleman hires this brougham from our livery every Wednesday morning to come to his office here. I'll be here on Wednesday again."

Dinah clutched his arm. "So will I," she said breathlessly.

She drank in his eyes for one last moment, then turned and ran toward the factory, her heart hammering with hope.

THE SHAMED LITTLE MATCH GIRL

DESPITE THE EXHAUSTION that had crept deep into her bones, Dinah was almost skipping as she turned down the pretty street to the widow's house that night. She felt as though she had floated through her shift at the match factory on a glorious tide of joy and hope. The sheer sight of Benjamin's eyes, the sound of his voice, had filled her with something bubbling and wonderful and free.

Seven more nights. In just seven more nights, she was going to be waiting for him in front of that office, and she would run into his arms and tell him everything that had happened. She knew that he and Aggie and Pearl would help her and Ollie. They had helped them even during much harder times, and the look in Benjamin's eyes had told Dinah that he had been telling the truth when he told her that he had never stopped thinking about her.

"Ollie," she called, pushing open the door to the basement. "You'll never believe who I saw in the street this..."

Her words died on her lips. Ollie was sitting on Aimee's sleeping pallet, an arm wrapped around the older girl, who had beat her home. The stoniness had vanished from Aimee's face, the ice from her eyes; she was a hunched figure now, her knees drawn up to her chest, face buried in her hands. And from her chest bubbled great, wet, desperate sobs that shook her entire body with their force.

Dinah felt everything inside her grow cold. "Ollie," she croaked, pulling the door shut behind her.

Ollie looked up. His eyes were full of tears, and he leaned his head against Aimee, rubbing her shoulder gently in a soothing motion.

"What's happened?" Dinah asked, hurrying over to the pallet and kneeling in front of Aimee. "Oh, Aimee, tell me what's wrong."

Aimee lifted her face from her hands. Her eyes were bloodshot, her face red and smeared with tears. "She's dead," she whispered.

The way she spoke those words sent an awful chill down Dinah's spine. "Wh-who?" she stammered. "Who's dead, Aimee?"

"Mrs. Mayhew," Aimee choked out. "The widow." She covered her face with her hands again. "I – I came home and went upstairs to polish her grate like I always do on a Wednesday night, and she was lying on the kitchen floor like she'd just toppled over in the middle of her baking. She's dead, Dinah. She's stone-cold dead." Her sobs returned with renewed vigor.

"Oh, Aimee, I'm so sorry." Dinah rested a hand on Aimee's shoulder. "She was one of the only friends you had."

"She was kind to me." Aimee cried. "I never knew my father, and my mother left me on a workhouse doorstep when I was a baby. She was the only person who's ever been kind to me, and now she's gone." She lifted her face from her hands again. "And oh, Dinah, where are we going to go? Her children are hateful. They'll take the house. They'll never let us stay here."

Dinah felt suddenly cold to the very marrow of her bones.

"We have to get away from here," said Aimee. "We can't come back here tomorrow night. Her body will be discovered. *We'll be discovered.*"

Ollie stared up at her with wide, terrified eyes. "What are we going to do?" he gasped.

Dinah looked to Aimee and saw Ollie's fear reflected in the older girl's eyes.

CHAPTER 10

The next day's shift at the match factory was the longest of Dinah's life. It was, as always, from six to ten; but every second seemed to drag, every intolerable minute slithering past with inexpressible slowness. Dinah had to spend the whole day trying her best not to glance over to the match-packaging machine, where Ollie was once again cowering under the clanking metal monster as the smaller match girls fed it bundles of finished matches to cut and bind.

She listened to Aimee sniffing quietly beside her, and knew that this time, it wasn't because of the poisonous fumes that rose to greet them every time they bent over that noxious vat of red phosphorous. Aimee's heart was truly shattered.

Even when their shift was over and Ollie slipped out from under the machine to creep outside with the girls, Aimee stayed very close to Dinah, their elbows almost touching as they walked out onto the street. The other match girls dispersed at once, heading straight to their tenements and the abandoned warehouses where they cowered in drafty corners, their eyes blank and exhausted. Only Ollie, Aimee, and Dinah were left standing on the sidewalk in front of the factory.

They had nowhere to go. The widow's family had already come to her house; everything they owned was once again in a sack over Dinah's shoulder.

"What do we do now?"

Dinah turned. It was Aimee who had asked the question. Her eyes were wide and swimming with tears, her face filled with pain and terror. It was impossible not to forgive her for the abuse she'd rained on Dinah in the past few months. Dinah reached out and put an arm around the girl's shoulders, pulling her close.

"Now we have to find somewhere to sleep," she said.

She led them to an alley they passed every morning on the way to work; it was normally unoccupied, and tonight was no different. There were a few puddles of rainwater in the back, but Ollie and Aimee dragged some broken boxes across them, and they managed to find a spot that was mostly dry. Wrapped in the only two blankets they owned, the children lay down in a row with Ollie in the middle. He draped a skinny arm over Dinah's waist and slept instantly.

Dinah herself was not so fortunate. She stared out at the mouth of the alley, at the splash of pale light that the nearest streetlamp offered, and she thought of Ollie and his tutor. She couldn't let him stop learning. Yet how would George tutor him now? How would they survive, without a place to live, without passing by the market square every night on their way home to get money and food from Mr. Hughes?

She squeezed her eyes shut, her exhausted body begging for sleep to come, her mind running too fast for sleep to catch up. One thing was for certain: even if she could convince Aimee to share a tenement with them, there was no possible way for their match girl salaries to afford rent, food, and Ollie's education. Without Mr. Hughes, there would have been no education for Ollie in the first place; and if they had to pay for rent, there would be hardly any money for food at all.

Her thoughts took her back to that awful Sunday night with Scully. The very memory turned her stomach, and yet, if she had accepted his offer, she and Ollie would still have a tenement to call home. There would be money for food and for learning. It had all seemed so appalling to her then, but she felt hardened by the past few months. Perhaps now that she knew the alternative, it would seem different once she looked it in the eye.

She could face her thoughts no longer. Pushing aside the blanket gently, she rolled to her feet. Ollie didn't stir, and she tucked the blanket around him, kissing him on the forehead. For a long moment, she sat staring at him where he slept.

"There's nothing I wouldn't do for you," she whispered.

Ollie didn't wake, but Dinah felt the truth of those words echoing down into her soul. She turned and walked out of the alley, her steps purposeful despite her tired muscles. It wasn't long before she'd left the warehouses behind and reached the paved streets of the district where Scully had brought her not so long ago. Despite the late hour, she could still hear merry carousing coming from the nearby public house; the fake diamond was still in the pawn shop window.

And the brothel was still well-lit and busy. Dinah stuck to the shadows, reluctant to be seen, and paused to stare at the neat little building. The hubbub of conversation coming from within made her skin crawl even though she couldn't make out any of the words. Yet, compared to the match factory, it looked positively inviting. At least in there, there were no poisonous fumes to inhale. It looked warm. There was more money than she'd ever had in her life. She remembered the times when Mama used to come home with pouches of money, when they'd been able to afford not only fresh bread but also vegetables and tripe and rent.

Dinah leaned against a streetlamp, her head spinning. She imagined Ollie learning to read, to do sums, eventually finding a job as a clerk or a teacher. She imagined him never going to bed hungry ever again, never having to worry about having a roof over his head ever again. She imagined him marrying a nice girl and having money for the wedding...

Dinah clenched her fists. Maybe some things would be worth this, even though she could already feel her stomach heaving just looking at the brothel. She squared her shoulders and took a step forward into the street.

As she did so, the door of the brothel swung open, and a powdered, rouged, silk-clad beauty strode out onto the sidewalk. The girl was rosy-cheeked, with a perfect golden blond mane that fell in gorgeous ringlets over her bare shoulders. Her eyes were the same cornflower blue as her dress, which swooped down low over her chest and hung in artful shapes over her hips and corset. She was beautiful, and when two young men passed her on the way into the brothel, they let out a whoop that made her flash them a wide grin.

The grin faded the moment the young men had gone inside. The girl in the blue dress sank down onto the front steps of the brothel, burying her face in her hands. Her elegant white shoulders began to tremble.

Dinah realized this girl was wholeheartedly weeping. The soft, broken sound filled the whole street, a sharp contrast to the happy murmur coming from inside. It reached all the way down into the pit of Dinah's soul, and froze her to the very core.

She turned around and didn't simply walk away; she ran. Arms swinging, heart pounding, she realized that there was only one other option.

And it might just lead down a similar road.

***

Mr. Hughes was just coming out of the bakery when Dinah reached the market square. She hesitated on a corner, just out of his sight, as she watched him hold the door for a young mother with a babe in her arms who was approaching the building. He gave them his gentle smile, his eyes dwelling for a long moment on the baby as he held out a finger. The baby giggled and reached for his finger with a chubby fist, and Mr. Hughes gave a gentle, delighted laugh.

Dinah leaned her head against the wall where she was standing. Mr. Hughes had done so much for her and for Ollie, yet she still couldn't shake the feeling that he had some hidden agenda. Perhaps she had been a fool to sneak out of the match factory at lunchtime; she knew she faced dismissal at best. But she was desperate. She couldn't go back to struggling to feed Ollie and pay the rent, let alone thinking of an education for him. She had to give him a better life or else hers would be worth nothing in her eyes.

Looking back up at Mr. Hughes, she saw that he had turned and was proceeding down the sidewalk away from her, whistling cheerfully as he swung his walking stick. He was her

THE SHAMED LITTLE MATCH GIRL

only hope. She took a deep breath and started to follow him, walking briskly on her aching feet.

"Mr. Hughes." she called out.

He stopped at once, spinning around at the sound of her voice. His gentle features softened as soon as his eyes rested on her face. "Miss Shaw," he said, his tone touched with concern. "What's the matter? Shouldn't you be at work?"

His soft tone broke something inside her. She felt her eyes fill with tears and forced herself to blink them back.

"My dear Miss Shaw." Mr. Hughes took an alarmed few steps closer to her, stopping short a little distance away. "Do tell me whatever it is that is the matter. Is it your little brother? Is he ill?"

"No – no. Ollie's hiding. He's all right," said Dinah, feeling a rush of both terror and gratitude: what would she do if he really was ill? It made her all the more determined to go through with her plan, no matter how much it terrified her. "But oh, Mr. Hughes, I don't know what to do. We're in such a terrible, terrible fix."

"Calm yourself, my dear," said Mr. Hughes, taking Dinah gently by the elbow as tears continued to pour down her cheeks. "Come now – let's sit on that little bench by the sweet shop. I think some iced sherbet will restore your good humor, and then you can tell me everything."

Dinah had never had sherbet before, and it nearly stunned her with its strange flavor, but she did find the tears slowing down slightly as Mr. Hughes sat a few feet away from her on the bench and watched her with knitted brows. "Now," he said. "Tell me what's the matter."

"Mr. Hughes, it's just everything." Dinah put her cup aside and interlaced her fingers, staring down at them. "We've lost our home. Well, it wasn't really a home. We slept in a widow's basement. But she died, and her children inherited the house and won't let us stay there."

"I'm sorry to hear that," said Mr. Hughes.

"There's no money for rent." Dinah shook her head, feeling a tear drip off the end of her nose. "There's hardly any money for food; and worst of all, I've – well, I've found a tutor for Ollie, another little boy who can read. I give him all the money that you give me. But now I can't afford that anymore." Dinah felt the lump in her throat swelling. "I can't afford to give Ollie a better future *and* keep him safe and fed in the present."

"You have quite the dilemma," said Mr. Hughes.

Dinah summoned her courage. *I'd do anything for Ollie*, she reminded herself, lifting her eyes to Mr. Hughes'. *Anything.* "Sir, you have always been terribly kind to us," she said. "I... I never wanted to ask, but now I have no choice." She swallowed hard, seeing something change in his eyes. "Would... would you help us? We can work for you. We would be your servants. I'll scrub your floors and Ollie will clean your stables, if you would only help us." She broke down and began to sob helplessly.

"Miss Shaw, Miss Shaw." Mr. Hughes let out a long sigh, then reached over and rested one of his big, soft hands on Dinah's clenched fingers. She looked up, a little startled by his unexpected touch, and he drew his hand back again. His eyes searched hers, looking almost frightened. "Miss Shaw..." he said again, then paused. "I would never ask you to be my servant. But there is something I would like to offer you." He cleared his throat. "Something I want to ask you."

Dinah felt her heart thump, hard. This was just what she'd been afraid of. She got up quickly, pulling her hands into her skirt. "Wh-what?" she stammered.

"Miss Shaw," said Mr. Hughes, "I would very much like to make you my wife."

Wife. The word bounced off Dinah almost as if she didn't understand it at all. She stared at him for a long moment, trying to understand.

"I want nothing improper," said Mr. Hughes quickly, "although I hope that you would learn to love me, and that later, when you are older, our union would yield children. But my house is big and lonely. I traveled too much as a young man and never found a wife. Now I am alone, and I no longer want to be that way."

Dinah was already backing away, her hands entangled in her skirt. Mr. Hughes took a step nearer, talking quickly.

"I can give you a home, Miss Shaw, a beautiful home with everything you could ever need. Books and food and warmth and friends – you would have everything. Your little brother would stay with us, of course. He would have a tutor. He would go to school when he's old enough and then to university. Miss Shaw, your brother would have a future."

Those words stopped her dead in her tracks. She felt her breath catch in her throat. The vision she'd had, the vision of Ollie in a warm home with a good career, had just grown even bigger. If what Mr. Hughes said was true, Ollie could be more than just a clerk; he could be a lawyer or a doctor or an engineer. He could have everything that his low birth denied him.

"You can walk away if you like," said Mr. Hughes, his own eyes filling with tears. "But if you do, you shall never see me again."

Dinah closed her eyes and her heart fled at once to Benjamin, to the way she'd felt encircled in his arms. And she knew that this would be utter treachery to him. But as much as Benjamin wanted to help her, he would never be able to give Ollie what Mr. Hughes now promised.

And Ollie was all that Dinah had left to live for.

Her heart shattered as her mind was made up. She opened her eyes. "Yes, Mr. Hughes," she said. "I will marry you."

PART III

CHAPTER 11

Three Years Later

Dinah tucked her feet a little closer underneath her, feeling a chill run down her spine as she gazed out of the elegant bay window despite the golden fire leaping in the parlor hearth. Outside, sleet was coming down in a thick, gray curtain. It made her cold just to look at it, even though it had been three years since the last time she'd had to be outside in anything like this weather.

She lifted a hand from her embroidery and ran it over the diamond ring on her left ring finger. After all this time, she had grown used to the feel of it. It had startled her at first each time she touched it and felt its coldness, or accidentally knocked it against something and heard the hard sound. Yet there was something about it that still never quite seemed to fit.

The parlor door opened a crack, and Aimee stepped inside, stony-faced in her black-and-white maid's uniform. "Mr. Dickson would like to speak with you, ma'am," she said.

"Oh, Aimee, you know you don't need to call me that," said Dinah, sighing.

Aimee gave her a sullen glare. She was eighteen now; the past three years had only served to harden the angles of her face. Dinah wondered sometimes if she should have talked Bartholomew into hiring Aimee as a maid at all. He had refused to take her in and raise her as his own, like he had done with Ollie, so this had seemed to be the best way to give Aimee somewhere safe to stay. But the girl seemed to hate Dinah for it.

Realizing Aimee was still waiting for a response, she forced a smile. "Let him in, please," she said.

"Yes, ma'am," said Aimee, spitting the words like acid. She pulled the door open and stepped aside as Ollie's tutor came into the room. He was a balding man with long, sad whiskers, and Dinah had always liked him. "Mr. Dickson," she said warmly. "Can I offer you anything?"

"No thank you, ma'am." Mr. Dickson gave a little bow. "I must be on my way before this weather worsens, but I came here to inform you that your brother is learning beautifully. Why, I have seldom had the pleasure of teaching such a sharp-witted little boy of ten."

Dinah felt a warm flush of delight filling her heart, making that wedding ring feel suddenly as though it was not so out of place after all. "Oh, I'm so glad to hear that, Mr. Dickson," she said.

THE SHAMED LITTLE MATCH GIRL

"He reads and does his arithmetic just as well as any other boy his age," said Mr. Dickson, "despite his rough start." He smiled. "He will be more than ready to go to school in the autumn."

Dinah laid a hand on her heart. "I cannot express what that means to me," she said, acutely aware of how her accent had changed now that she spent so much time hanging onto Bartholomew's arm at the many business soirees he was constantly attending.

"I know." Mr. Dickson smiled kindly. "Now – I do apologize, Mrs. Hughes, but I should be going."

"Of course. Allow me to see you out," said Dinah, getting to her feet.

Abruptly, her vision blurred, black dots swarming in front of her eyes. She let out a gasp and grabbed at the nearest pillar to steady herself; her knees wobbled, and the world began to spin slightly. She heard a cry of alarm and felt Mr. Dickson's hand on her arm guiding her back to the seat by the bay window. When her hearing returned, he was bending over her, his worried eyes inches from her own.

"Mrs. Hughes." he cried. "Are you unwell?"

"No – no, Mr. Dickson," said Dinah, swallowing hard against a tide of nausea and terror rising in her belly. "I... I'm quite all right."

"You're deathly pale," said Mr. Dickson.

"I think I just need a little air," she said, as lightly as she could.

In reality, as she clung to Mr. Dickson's arm and allowed herself to be escorted into the little covered courtyard at the back of the house; she could feel herself shaking. The moment of weakness had passed, yet it was not the first she'd had in the past few months. The mornings were worst: she felt so sick then that she could hardly rise and prepare breakfast for Ollie and Bartholomew.

Mr. Dickson left her sitting on a bench in the courtyard and hurried off through the sleet. The air was very cold, but Dinah was warmly bundled in her coat and it only served to clear her spinning head. She would have to see a doctor, she decided quietly. But there was no need to disturb Ollie or Bartholomew. She didn't want Ollie to worry; and as for Bartholomew, while he had never yet been harsh with her even in their marriage bed once she had consented to go to it, he hardly ever seemed to hear a word she said to him these days.

There was movement in the garden opposite. Dinah spotted the muffled figures of the neighboring children hastening up the back path after their day at school; their mother, Mrs. Wentworth, was close behind them. Delighted by the sight of another woman, Dinah got up. Perhaps Mrs. Wentworth would know which doctor was best to see.

"Good afternoon." she called out, raising a hand.

Mrs. Wentworth shot her a quick glance and a curt nod, then hurried back into the house. Dinah sank back down onto her bench. She still hoped that one day she would win her neighbor over, even though Mrs. Wentworth – like all her other female neighbors – disapproved of Bartholomew's wedding to a little street waif like her.

It seemed that no one approved of his choice to marry her. Ollie's benefit from the decision would have to be her only reward.

THE SHAMED LITTLE MATCH GIRL

It was, in the end, old Mrs. Bates from across the road – the elder Mrs. Bates, mother of the lady of the house, who was so old and deaf that it didn't seem to matter to her whom Bartholomew had married – who pointed Dinah in the direction of the nearest physician. His offices turned out to be only two blocks away. Knowing that the coachman would tell Bartholomew about it if she commanded him to bring out the horses, Dinah decided that the best thing to do would be to simply walk there one Friday morning while Ollie was busy with his lessons.

It was a pretty morning, for January; a rare burst of sunshine had appeared from behind a thin veil of clouds, and there was only a gentle breeze as Dinah made her way along the quiet streets. She lifted her purse a little higher more out of habit than anything else. There were no pickpockets here. In fact, compared with this neighborhood, the street where the widow had lived – the one she considered to be the prettiest in the world – was one step above a slum itself. Here, there were horses with plumes on their bridles, and long gardens with green lawns in the summer stretching out in front of the houses. Those lawns were white and glittering with snow now, and there were children playing on some of them, making snowmen.

Dinah lifted her face to the sun and sighed, trying to cling to the warmth rising in her heart as she thought of Ollie. Once his lessons were finished, he, too, would be running around in the back garden with his friends, building snowmen and having snowball fights and later going to the park to ice skate on the pond. His cheeks were rosy, and his belly was full. And Bartholomew wasn't bad as a husband. He was kindly and would never raise a hand to Dinah, that much she knew for sure.

So why could she never stop thinking of Benjamin?

The memory of their last meeting flooded back to her, sweet and pure as the day it had happened. His smell. The light in those perfect, green eyes...

Dinah pushed the memory away, shaking her head as she reached over to touch the wedding ring on her finger. *You're married*, she reminded herself, a pit of guilt opening in her stomach. She couldn't go around hankering after other men like this.

She let out a sigh and turned the corner, and there was Benjamin walking briskly along the sidewalk in front of her, his red curls radiant in the sun.

Dinah stopped dead. A young man nearly walked into her and stumbled aside, cursing under his breath. She didn't care; she just stared. Benjamin was walking away from her, but there was no mistaking that elegant frame, those verdant curls. As she watched, he glanced into the street, and the profile was just as she had always remembered it. The line of his jaw still so noble. She imagined the color of his eyes would still be so pure. He looked well; his cheeks were rosy, his eyes bright, and he wore a well-cut coat that seemed impervious to the breeze.

"Benjamin." The word came out breathy and almost silent. Dinah took a staggering few steps forward, then launched into a run. His name rose in her throat, ready to leap out of her lips and make him turn around—

And then what? Dinah stuttered to a halt once more. Then what would she do, once she had Benjamin's attention? What would she say? What would he say, when he saw the ring on her finger?

Deep shame bloomed in her belly. The last time she'd seen Benjamin, she'd promised to see him again. And she never had. She had been too busy preparing to marry Bartholomew, a man she liked but could never love. She had betrayed the best friend she'd ever had, the one man for whom her heart still yearned.

Tears prickled at the back of her eyes. Lowering her head, Dinah kept walking, letting Benjamin get further and further away.

THE DOCTOR WAS A SMALL, dapper man with a fussy mustache and cold gray eyes. When Dinah came into his office, he was busy checking his pocket watch, and he barely glanced up at her as she gently closed the door behind her.

"You'll be Mrs. Hughes," he said.

"Yes, Dr. Holt," said Dinah nervously.

"Sit. I do prefer to make house calls, you know," said Dr. Holt.

Dinah perched unhappily on the edge of a chair by the doctor's desk. "I understand, sir. I just didn't want to bother my husband with this. I think it's nothing."

"Yet you still choose to bother me," sighed Dr. Holt.

Dinah felt like she'd been slapped. She closed her lips, deciding not to breathe another word lest he throw her clean out of the office. It seemed that, while many things had changed for her once she'd left the streets, she would still seem to some to be invisible or somehow inhuman just because she was a woman and had lived on the streets.

The doctor dropped his watch back into his pocket and opened the black bag on his desk. "What has been the matter, Mrs. Hughes?" he asked.

"I feel ill in the early mornings," said Dinah, "and sometimes terribly weak and dizzy."

"I see," said Dr. Holt. He laid his fingers on her pulse, listened to her chest, and then gently probed her belly with his fingers. They were surprisingly quick and tender through her dress; she had almost expected his hands to be as hard as his voice. "And when last have you had your monthly sickness?" he asked delicately.

Dinah shifted uncomfortably on her chair. "Ah – not for the past two months," she admitted. "But this has happened before." She swallowed. In fact, in her time on the streets, it had been more common not to suffer her monthly ailment than to actually have it.

"And you come from a hard childhood, Mrs. Hughes?" asked Dr. Holt.

"Y-yes, sir," said Dinah.

"Then you may have experienced the failure of the menses thanks to poor nutrition," he said, "but this is not the case now." He stepped back. "Have you ever been with child?"

With child? It took Dinah a moment to realize what he was saying. "No, sir," she said.

"Then congratulations are in order," said Dr. Holt. "You are expecting your firstborn."

THE SHAMED LITTLE MATCH GIRL

Perhaps it was only her imagination, but as Dinah set the tureen of roast vegetables down on the long table in the dining room, she felt something stir in her belly. It was less of a kick and more of a tiny, wriggling movement, not unpleasant, but very much startling.

"Oh," she gasped, nearly dropping the tureen. It wobbled in her hands, but somehow, she managed to put it down on the table without spilling anything.

"Oh, Dinah," sighed Bartholomew, giving her a glance from his spot at the head of the table. "Why must you be so clumsy?"

"I'm sorry, darling," said Dinah nervously. The word felt stilted and silly on her lips; she only said it because Bartholomew had requested it about a year into their marriage. It was probably the same time that he started to realize how much she didn't love him.

Bartholomew shook his head. "Sit, please," he ordered.

Dinah took her place opposite Ollie, who gave her a wide-eyed look. She smiled broadly to reassure him as she spooned vegetables onto Bartholomew's china plate. "How did your lessons go today, Ollie?" she asked.

"Very well, thank you," said Ollie. He smiled. Sometimes he looked so different than the little boy Dinah had fought for out on those streets; his wild curls had been trimmed, and the pinched look was gone from his face, making his eyes look smaller. Even his speech had completely changed. Yet there was nothing different in his smile, nothing at all. "We learned some history today," he added. "I learned about the Hundred Years' War."

"Oh, that's very good." Bartholomew grinned at Ollie, his eyes filling with a warmth that Dinah never saw anymore when he looked at her. "Did you know that one of my ancestors fought in the war?"

"He did?" said Ollie, wide-eyed.

"Oh, yes," said Bartholomew. "He was quite the hero, too. He was there at the Battle of Tours."

"I didn't know that," said Ollie, deeply impressed.

They continued to chatter as Dinah picked at her food. Once, she would have gobbled every morsel; now, she found herself privately wishing for custard for some inexplicable reason even though she was faced with a perfectly good dish of roast beef and vegetables. She forced another bite of potato down her throat.

It had been a month since she had visited the doctor. She was starting, now, to notice the growing bulge in her midriff; Dr. Holt had advised her to wear looser clothing, and she had hoped that Bartholomew would ask why when she had asked him for money to go to the milliner's. But he hadn't asked. He'd just given her what she wanted, like he always did, almost without meeting her eyes. It was as if he hadn't even noticed that she no longer wore corsets.

As if she had become completely invisible to him.

Dinah felt like screaming. She couldn't tell Ollie yet, not before telling Bartholomew. She couldn't tell Aimee – what point would there be? All she'd get from her was criticism. None of her neighbors wanted to know. She'd tried to tell old Mrs. Bates, but the old lady had fallen asleep at that point in their conversation.

There was only one thing for it. She couldn't keep her excitement and terror bottled up any longer. As soon as Ollie had finished his dinner and asked to be excused, Dinah turned to Bartholomew, tangling her hands in a napkin to hide their shaking.

"Bartholomew, there's something I need to tell you," she said.

Bartholomew shot her a glance as he poured himself another glass of red wine. "Yes?"

"Darling." Dinah cleared her throat over the awkward word. "Please – listen to me."

Bartholomew set down the bottle and stared at her. "I *am* listening, Dinah," he said with a slight edge to his voice. "Why would you think I wasn't?"

Dinah pushed aside the hurt and confusion that always greeted her after one of his increasingly frequent irritable outbursts. She reached over and laid a hand over his. "We're going to have a baby, Bartholomew," she said.

His eyes widened. A burst of joy and gentleness filled them, lighting them up so brightly that Dinah's heart beat faster. "A baby?" he cried. "When?"

"In the spring," said Dinah.

"Oh, Dinah." Bartholomew raised both hands to his mouth, his eyes filling with joyous tears. "Oh, I'm going to be a father. I'm finally going to be a father."

Dinah grinned in response to his cry of joy, but a note of pain was struck deep in her heart. She had never been able to make him so happy by herself. She remembered his words the day he'd proposed to her: *I hope that... our union would yield children.* Was this all he'd really wanted from her?

"Dinah, my love, my precious." Bartholomew got up and wrapped his arms around her with a tenderness she hadn't felt from him for months and months. "Oh, what a glorious gift, my darling."

Dinah returned his embrace, hungry for the soothing contact it gave her. Yet part of her heart felt like it had been trodden upon. In truth, she was afraid. She had no idea how she was going to bring this baby into the world with not a female friend to her name.

CHAPTER 12

THE MIDWIFE WAS a formidable person with a jawline like an anvil and great craggy brows. Dinah would not have been particularly surprised to see tusks protruding from her bottom jaw like some kind of fabled ogre, but to her surprise, the midwife's smile revealed two dimples in her stern cheeks. It was almost jolly.

"Hello there, dear," she said, even though she really should have been addressing Dinah as 'ma'am'.

"G-good morning," said Dinah nervously. She laid a hand on the great curve of her belly, willing the tiny life inside to do something – to kick or turn over or do any of the little movements that had become part of her daily life over the past few months.

"Now, I expect we're not delivering a baby today, are we?" The midwife gave another sweet smile as she set her bag down on the parlor table. She knelt down in front of the chaise where Dinah was sitting and patted her knee. "What seems to be the matter?"

Beside Dinah, Bartholomew leaned over, putting a protective arm around Dinah's shoulders. "Now I won't stand for any snide remarks from you, Mrs. Thistlewit," he said. "This is our firstborn child, and we are very proud expectant parents. Everything simply *must* go smoothly."

Mrs. Thistlewit gave Bartholomew a surprised look. "Now, sir," she said, her jaw jutting a little again, "don't you think that any child matters the less to me for being a second-born, or for being the child of a parlor-maid or a street picker, for all that matter. I'll care for your wife and little one like I care for any of them."

Dinah felt Bartholomew bristle. "Now see here..." he began.

"Two days," said Dinah quickly, to break his tirade. "I haven't felt the baby move for two days."

Mrs. Thistlewit's eyes widened in a way that made terror spring in Dinah's heart. Bartholomew leapt up from the chaise, letting out a howl of agony.

"What? What's this? Why didn't you tell me?" he cried, covering his face with his hands and lumbering around the room like some large bull stung by a bee. "My poor, poor little baby." He began to weep like a child.

Mrs. Thistlewit gave him another startled look. "Stop that at once," she cried. "You don't know there's anything the matter with your child just yet."

Bartholomew sank back down onto the chaise, his eyes wide and swimming with tears. It was a startling sight to Dinah. She had never seen a grown man cry until she'd become pregnant; now it seemed to happen to Bartholomew with increasing frequency. Yet as sweet and tender as he had become toward the baby, so harsh and prickly and nervous had he become toward Dinah.

"You don't understand," he mumbled. "Nothing can happen to this child. It's my only reason for living."

"Don't be so dramatic," said Mrs. Thistlewit firmly. She turned back to Dinah. "Now, my dear, there's no reason for you to panic just yet. Have you had any bleeding?"

"None," said Dinah meekly.

"That's good," said Mrs. Thistlewit. "When do you normally feel the little one kick?"

Dinah paused. "After drinking something," she said. "It always moves when I've just had something cold to drink." She ran a hand over her belly.

"Good." Mrs. Thistlewit got up. "We'll give you a glass of cold water, and then we'll see what happens."

Bartholomew turned. Aimee was lurking in the corner of the parlor, dusting the china decorations over the mantelpiece. "You," he barked. "Please fetch a glass of cold water. Now."

Dinah cringed at his harsh tone. "Please, Aimee," she added softly.

Aimee shot her a furious glance before storming off. Dinah had to fight back tears. How had she become so terribly alone?

A few moments later, Aimee returned, bearing the glass of water on a tray and utter hatred in her cold eyes. She held out the tray, and Dinah gripped the glass, feeling her heart pound with fear.

"Try not to excite yourself, dear," said Mrs. Thistlewit. "Remember what it could do to your little one."

"Yes. Stop that nervousness at once, Dinah," snapped Bartholomew. "You know that any kind of passion could cause all kinds of trouble with my child."

It's my child, too, Dinah thought, aching inside. She forced a smile, pretending to relax as she sipped the water.

"Do you feel anything?" asked Mrs. Thistlewit.

Dinah laid a hand on her belly. She could feel her heart freeze as she waited. Then, there was a tiny flutter. Was it a kick? It could have been. She shot a glance at Bartholomew and saw the fear in his eyes as he glared at her. All he wanted was this baby. If she couldn't give him that...

The flutter came again. She wasn't sure what it was, but she had to believe it was the little one. She smiled widely, turning back to Mrs. Thistlewit. "It moved," she cried. "The baby moved."

Bartholomew seemed too overcome with relief for words. He buried his face in his hands and sat there trembling, breathing hard.

Dinah forced a smile onto her face. "See, darling?" she said, touching his shoulder. "Everything is just fine."

But she wasn't so sure. And looking into Mrs. Thistlewit's eyes, she knew the midwife wasn't so sure either.

"Well, that's good," said Mrs. Thistlewit warily. "Still, Mrs. Hughes, I think you need to begin preparing your home for your confinement. We would rather not take any chances, would we? You should begin your confinement a little early."

Dinah felt her heart droop. She knew she was about to spend weeks upon weeks trapped in this house, alone and friendless —except for her young brother.

"Do you have someone who can come to help you?" asked Mrs. Thistlewit. "Your mother or sister, perhaps."

"No," said Dinah. She thought of Mama and her belly squeezed with shame. "No one."

"Then I will help you," said Mrs. Thistlewit, giving her leg another little pat. "I'll be back on Monday at noon to help you prepare your home."

A rush of gratitude flooded through Dinah. "Oh, thank you, Mrs. Thistlewit."

"Yes, thank you," said Bartholomew, raising a tear-streaked face from his hands. "This child – it's everything to me."

Dinah looked into his desperate eyes and felt fear rising in her.

She absolutely had to deliver this baby. She dared not imagine the consequences if she failed.

※

Monday morning came beautifully sunny after a weekend of cold and rain. As Aimee cleared away the breakfast dishes and Dinah followed Bartholomew into the parlor, she couldn't resist going over to the bay window, peering out into the sunlit garden. There was no grass on the lawn yet, just ice that shimmered in the sunlight, a few snowdrops raising their shy heads from among it; the streets were busy with happy people walking or driving or riding to and fro, and Dinah felt her heart lift at the sight.

It was seldom that anything seemed capable of making her really happy these days. As if in response, she felt another tiny, fluttering movement in her belly. She laid a hand over it, heartened by the little movement, even though it was still much weaker than what she'd experienced in the past few months.

"Bartholomew, darling," she said, turning to him, "I think I shall go to the market this morning. I need a few things for my confinement. It'll be quick – I'll be home long before Mrs. Thistlewit is here to help me prepare the house."

"To the market?" Bartholomew swung around. "Come away from that bay window at once, Dinah. Are you insane? The market is two blocks away. It's far too much exertion for a woman in your condition, and far too cold out. You'll catch your death and put my child at risk."

Something in his tone of voice made something snap inside her. "I'm about to spend weeks trapped inside this house," she cried. "Let me have one more hour of freedom."

"Freedom? Dinah, you're being foolish," countered Bartholomew. He plopped into his armchair and took his newspaper from its place on the coffee table. "Send Aimee if you need anything. The girl is so sullen that it's unpleasant to have her in the house."

Dinah couldn't deny that, yet still she found herself incapable of letting go of the hope of just an hour outside in the sun. "No, please," she said.

Bartholomew looked up at her, his eyebrows rising. "I beg your pardon?" he said.

"I know you don't want me anymore, Bartholomew," said Dinah, her voice dropping. "I know you likely never did. You only wanted this baby. But I'm still a person with hopes and needs and emotions."

"Far too many of those," snapped Bartholomew. "You're becoming hysterical. You'll injure our child."

"Then let me walk to the market," said Dinah, folding her arms over the bulge of her belly. "Perhaps that will ease the hysteria."

She saw his face soften just slightly and drove home her advantage. "Please, darling," she wheedled. "I can't stand it. I shall fly into a passion of dismay if I can't have one last walk in the sun."

Bartholomew sighed, looking back to his paper. "Fine. But I can't go with you right now as I must do my daily reading. So, you will walk slowly," he said. "And you will be back soon."

"Yes, darling, I will," said Dinah, relief flooding her heart.

A few moments later, she was already feeling better as she strode along in the bright sunlight, careful not to walk too briskly thanks to the ice that lay in the shaded corners of the street. She took a few deep breaths, feeling herself calm. She knew that resting a hand on her belly would seem immodest in a busy street, so she contented herself with smiling down at it instead. *It's going to be all right, little one*, she told the unborn child and herself. *We're going to be all right.*

It had to be true. And if she just stayed calm, and stayed inside during her confinement, perhaps it would be. Perhaps those feeble little kicks meant nothing at all. She would have a happy, healthy baby in her arms in a few months' time, and Bartholomew might even love her again. It was strange how much she wanted that, even though she knew she could never love him.

As she turned into the market square, inexplicably, there he was again: the only man in the world that Dinah could ever love, the only one she had ever loved. She froze in place, her empty shopping basket swinging on her arm. Benjamin was standing by a stall selling fresh vegetables. It must be warmer somewhere in the country, for the carrots were a fresh, verdant orange, their tops richest green, yet surely pale in comparison with the hue of his eyes as he smiled at the vendor and handed over his money.

Shame billowed inside Dinah's heart. This man, with his sweet smile, with his gentle eyes, with his red curls glowing like a halo around his face – this was the man she had left on that street to wait for her. That had been more than three years ago now. Was his heart still broken?

She stepped back, ready to simply turn around and go home, but before she could turn away his eyes lifted and somehow, across the bustle of the square, they found hers. For a moment that seemed to last much too long. She felt the warmth of them penetrate the deepest and most frozen corners of her heart.

His voice floated up to meet her. "Dinah," he cried.

Dinah forced herself to smile. Holding her basket in front of her round belly, she stepped across the square, her strides eager even as her heart ached for what she'd done to him. "Benjamin," she cried.

He was striding toward her, his arms held out as though he would snatch her up into them and spin her around the way he had done on that glorious morning so long ago. When he was a few yards away, though, she saw his eyes drop to her belly. He stopped short, lifting them to hers once more, and she saw agony in them.

THE SHAMED LITTLE MATCH GIRL

That was when she knew that he was not merely excited to see an old friend. Inside the pain she saw in Benjamin's eyes, she knew he still loved her.

She turned to go, but he reached out, grasping her elbow with a gentle finger. "Dinah, don't go," he said. "You look so well."

She looked back up at him; it was like looking into the sun – warm, yet painful. "S-so do you," she stammered, realizing it was true. He was wearing a cloth cap cocked at a jaunty angle, and a well-cut coat with a warm scarf knotted around his throat. His cheeks had a healthy, well-fleshed tinge to them that only made him all the more handsome.

"Ah, yes," said Benjamin softly. "I'm very well." He let go of her elbow, stepping back. "How are you?"

She resisted the urge to cover her ring with her hand. "Oh, I'm fine." she said, as brightly as she could. "What are you doing these days? Are you still working for the livery yard?"

"Oh, no, not anymore." Benjamin grinned widely. "Another livery stable – a more expensive one with rich clients – has hired me now."

"Benjamin, that's wonderful." This time there was no need for Dinah to feign her enthusiasm. "I'm so glad for you. It must be wonderful to be a groom in such a prestigious place."

"No, no." Benjamin laughed. "Well, it would be, but I'm stable master now."

"Stable master?" Dinah laughed with delight. "That's the best thing I've heard for a long time. I'm so happy for you. You deserve every bit of the joy you have right now."

Benjamin's eyes softened, and Dinah realized again just how deep they were. She forced herself to look away, to picture

Bartholomew instead. He was her husband; she owed him all the loyalty she had, even if her heart still yearned after Benjamin with a passion so intense it took her breath away.

"And you, Dinah?" Benjamin asked softly. "You look so well. I'm glad to see you wearing such nice clothes."

Dinah ran a hand over the rich fabric of her favorite new blue dress. "I..." She cleared her throat. "Well, I'm married, Benjamin."

"I see." He smiled gently. "Does he treat you well?"

His words made her heart shatter. She knew he felt betrayed, she had seen the pain in his eyes, and yet he had no accusations to make; all he wanted was to care for her. Just as he had always done, since they were little children in neighboring tenements, scrambling to find enough food to eat.

"Y-yes," she stammered out. Suddenly she had to get away from him, to escape the reality of what she had done to him. "Yes, he's – he's very good to me. I'm sorry. I have to go."

"Dinah..." Benjamin began.

She heard his voice crack on her name and could no longer bear to be near him without throwing her arms around him. She spun around and broke into a jog, desperate to calm herself, to get away. The street home beckoned to her. She sped up, hastening through the shadow of one of the stalls, and that was when disaster struck.

Her foot struck a patch of ice. It slipped, and Dinah let out a cry, throwing out her arms to catch herself. Her shopping basket fell to the cobbles and broke apart. She snatched at the edge of the stall and felt it slide through her fingers. She scrambled to regain her feet and felt them slither on the ice. All she could think of was her child, her baby, and the way her belly was rushing down toward the unyielding ground.

She heard cries around her. She heard her own scream, felt the wrench in her shoulder as she turned, desperately trying to save her baby. For a moment, she thought she had succeeded.

Then she met the ground, hip and shoulder first, and rolled right onto her belly even as she threw her arms around it for protection. She felt the grinding of the small bones in her hands as she rolled, felt the pang of agony run all the way to the pit of her womb, and lay still, curled around her belly.

People were shouting, running to her. She knew only agony, yet the deep pain in her belly could not hope to equal the hopeless shattering of her heart. Benjamin was beside her, rolling her onto her back, his hands on her shoulders, his frightened eyes on hers. He was speaking, saying the same words over and over. "It'll be all right. You'll be all right."

He kept saying it even when the doctor had already come, when he had been pushed aside, when Dr. Holt's cold hands were on her cheeks, his voice telling her to say something. But Dinah could say nothing. She could only hear Benjamin somewhere in the background, still telling her that it would be all right.

But she felt the wetness on the inside of her thighs and the pain in the pit of her belly.

And she knew that it was not going to be all right.

※

DINAH DID NOT SEE her baby. Dr. Holt kept telling her to close her eyes, to rest, that it was over, that she would live.

All she wanted to do was to see her baby. To hold it. To hear its cry.

But it would never cry.

※

Dinah lay in bed for nine days. In that time, the only people she saw were Dr. Holt and Mrs. Thistlewit and Aimee. Dr. Holt was cold; Aimee spoke not a single word when she brought Dinah the meals she didn't want and the drinks she had no appetite for. Mrs. Thistlewit held her when she sobbed, stroking her braided hair with the empathy of a woman who had seen a thousand babies lost, and knew she would see a thousand more.

It was only when Dinah was allowed to leave her bed and stumble over to the sofa on aching legs that felt weak and useless that Mrs. Thistlewit agreed to allow Bartholomew into the room. The midwife gave Dinah a look of deep sympathy before letting herself out into the hallway to call Bartholomew.

Dinah lay on the sofa, her head on some pillows that Mrs. Thistlewit had arranged there for her and gazed out of the window. She knew she shouldn't be getting too much light, or at least, that was what Dr. Holt had said; but she had begged and begged until Mrs. Thistlewit had opened the curtains just enough for her to see out onto the street. She tried to think of other things. Of the meticulously tended little crocuses blooming in a window box across the street. Of Benjamin. But even that could not hold her attention. It was all utterly consumed by the agony that still lingered in her body, and the far worse, far more piecing pain that filled her heart.

She felt completely empty. She felt robbed.

THE SHAMED LITTLE MATCH GIRL

She had truly wanted the baby that she had just lost, and she knew that she would give anything – anything in the world – simply to have a healthy child wriggling in her arms. And she knew that as much as she wanted the baby, Bartholomew had wanted it so much more.

Fear curled in her stomach. She knew he would blame her for losing the baby; after all, he'd told her not to go. Would it be enough that he would drive her away? Would she and Ollie be on the streets again, alone and friendless, steeped in shame?

The door creaked. Dinah looked up as Bartholomew came in, and she barely recognized the man she had married. His usually neat hair stood every which way; his beard was mussed, as if he had fallen asleep on some hard surface. His face was blotched red and purple, and his eyes so red that she could barely see their pure color at all.

"Bartholomew, darling," she whispered.

"Darling?" Bartholomew stared at her, his hands hanging limply by his sides. "Darling? How dare you call me by such endearments when I know that there is nothing in your heart for me but hatred."

He didn't raise his voice, but the words still slammed into her skin like blows. Dinah felt tears rising to her eyes. "Please," she began.

"No. Do not plead with me. Not after what you have done." Bartholomew's voice cracked, and he raised a trembling finger to point at her. "You lost my child. Your recklessness, your irresponsibility took away the life of the one thing I had left to live for."

"I'm so sorry," said Dinah, tears pouring down her cheeks. "I never meant..."

"You're a fool," cried Bartholomew. "You've taken everything from me, you worthless girl. I should have left you on the streets that I saved you from." His eyes flashed.

"Please, Bartholomew," Dinah begged, sobbing hysterically. "Please, forgive me. For Ollie's sake. Oh, please, don't…"

Bartholomew's face twisted. For a second, Dinah thought it was in anger, and cowered against the settee in fear of what he was about to say to her. Then, his mouth fell open, and he let out a small, desperate, choking sound.

"B-Bartholomew?" Dinah breathed.

Bartholomew clutched a hand over his chest and reached for the nearby sideboard to steady himself, his knees buckling.

"Bartholomew!" Dinah flew up from the sofa.

It was too late. He had already crumpled to the floor with a terrible, dull thud. Dinah found herself beside him, her hands searching his familiar face, turning him onto his back. "Oh, darling, talk to me," she gasped. "Wake up."

Bartholomew let out a groan. There were running feet in the hallway, and the door wrenched open; Mrs. Thistlewit ran inside with Aimee hot on her heels. Aimee pulled Dinah to her feet and dragged her away from her fallen husband as Mrs. Thistlewit crouched beside him.

And Dinah knew was that nothing was going to be the same again.

PART IV

CHAPTER 13

One Year Later

Dinah gazed at her reflection in the window. Winter had decorated it with delicate bursts of silvery frost, twirling and stretching across the glass, as if intricately painted there by some diligent hand. Her reflection shimmered among them, barely visible through the frost and the black veil of mourning that hung over her face. She could just glimpse her red eyes, her pinched cheeks.

She looked so much older than her eighteen years. She *felt* so much older.

The tirade coming from behind her was little help in making her heart feel lighter. She closed her eyes for a minute, listening, even though each word felt like it was adding another few years to her age.

"This house is far too big for you in any case, Dinah. What will you do with all these rooms? You'll be overwhelmed. It would be for the best."

Dinah let out a sigh and turned around. Bartholomew's brother, Geoffrey, was sitting in her late husband's armchair. Part of her wanted to seize his arm and wrench him out of the chair where Bartholomew had always sat in the evenings, enjoying a pipe and a book, his two greatest joys. A deep pang ran through her heart. She searched Geoffrey's face, hoping perhaps to find some vestige of Bartholomew there, some glimpse of the man that she had grown to love a little despite it all.

But Geoffrey was nothing like his brother. His flat, red face held small black eyes that glinted with meanness; there was a looseness around his lips, a redness of his nose that hinted at the excesses he enjoyed enough to make his well-cut waistcoat bulge into his lap. Bartholomew had been harsh with her in his last year, but he had been a gentleman always. And as for Geoffrey, Dinah had known street sweepers who were more of a gentleman than this well-bred pig.

"I have been living in this house for the six months since your brother passed on, Geoffrey," said Dinah calmly, "and have yet to feel in the least overwhelmed."

"Even with your maid having married and gone?" asked Geoffrey.

Dinah had expected to be hurt when Aimee had told her she was leaving, yet all she'd felt was relief. "I have hired another maid," she said.

"Surely you can't dream of affording that," scoffed Geoffrey.

"Actually, I can," said Dinah. "Bartholomew made sure that I would be comfortable." She felt a pang run through her at those words – a pang of intolerable guilt. Every day when she awoke in the four-poster bed they had shared, when she dined on the hearty meals that her inheritance was paying for, when she thought of Ollie at the prestigious school whose costs Bartholomew's estate covered, she felt it again.

Because she had killed him. Even cold Dr. Holt had tried to be kind to her, to tell her that Bartholomew died of hysteria, of apoplexy. But she knew better. She knew he had died of a broken heart because she had lost his child.

And looking into Geoffrey's angry little eyes, she knew that he knew it, too.

"I can't believe my brother's foolishness," he spat. "To marry a street waif in the first place. He dishonored the family name. And then to leave everything to you in his will, after you lost his child and caused the grief that killed him."

Dinah took in a sharp breath. Geoffrey might just as surely have plunged a dagger into her heart.

"He left nothing to me, his own brother. *Nothing*." Geoffrey spat on a fine spray of saliva. "You bewitched him, you saucy little minx. You did something to my brother to addle his fine mind. He was a gentleman until he met you. And now, look."

Dinah felt her eyes fill with tears. "What would you have me do?" she cried.

"Leave," said Geoffrey simply. "Go and live somewhere smaller. A cottage. Bartholomew would have wanted that much – even I must concede that. Leave the rest of the house and estate to me, his only surviving relative, the way it should always have been." He folded his arms over his paunch.

"You know I can't do that," said Dinah. "What would become of Ollie?"

At the mention of Ollie's name, Geoffrey's eyes softened, the way everyone's did when she mentioned her sweetly charming little brother.

"Well, that's another matter," he mumbled. "The child is at boarding school most of the time. My brother formally adopted him, after all. He is well provided for. He would stay here during the holidays with Letitia and I."

Dinah stared at him. Geoffrey's wife was a wispy, mousy little thing, easily pushed around by her husband's boorish personality, but she had a good heart and had always been good to Ollie. "Do you mean that?" she said.

Geoffrey's eyes glinted with opportunity. "Oh, yes," he said. "Of course. Oliver belongs here. None of this is his fault." His eyes darkened. "It's yours. You are the one who should not be allowed to stay in the house of the man who you killed."

His words lanced through her to the core, and not because of his hard eyes or his heartless voice or his awful manner, but because she believed them with all her heart to be true.

THE COTTAGE WAS PLEASANT ENOUGH, Dinah supposed. One of the bankers who had managed Bartholomew's affairs turned out to be kinder than Dinah had expected, and although he had tried to persuade her to stay in Bartholomew's house as his will decreed, he had eventually given in and helped her to find a place whose rent she could afford. He had been appalled when she had told him that she only wanted two months' worth of rent from Bartholomew's account.

"But Mrs. Hughes," he had said, appalled, "you would have to find work."

After so much time spent alone in that great empty house, Dinah could think of nothing better than being busy. "Yes," she had said. "I look forward to it."

The horrified banker had spoken to his cousin, a glover, and that was how Dinah found herself working at the front desk of the glover's shop. Her reading was still not particularly good, but she could do a few sums and read the labels on the gloves, and that would have to do.

It was half an hour before she was due to be at work at ten minutes to eight. Dinah sat alone in her little kitchen, picking at the bread and jam she was having for breakfast. The bread was fresh, the jam, sweet; yet Dinah felt them turn to ashes on her tongue.

She sighed, gazing around the little kitchen. It was very bare, yet it was still a king's palace in comparison with the tenement where she and Ollie had grown up. She told herself that she should be happy. She had gotten everything that she wanted, after all: she had a full belly every night, a roof over her head, and a little brother who was doing very well at school. She would see him again soon for the Easter holidays, and perhaps he'd spend a few nights at her cottage before going back to being pampered by his adopted Aunt Letitia. What more could she ask for?

She lowered her head, her heart aching. Benjamin's kind face, his gentle smile, his shining eyes came into her mind, and she couldn't shake them off. He must still be running the livery stable somewhere nearby. It would be so easy to find him...

She shook her head, pushing her plate aside, and got up from the table. And what then? Someone as good and kind and charming as Benjamin would long since be married. And even if he wasn't, he had seen her shame. He had seen her lose her child. He couldn't possibly want her anymore.

It was time she accepted her loneliness and made herself content with the fact that Ollie was happy. It was all she had ever lived for. It would have to do, just like everything else.

※

THE GLOVER'S shop was on the same market square where Dinah had fallen on that awful, fateful day. Even though the warm tang of spring was rich in the air, Dinah could still not bring herself to cross that particular patch of the square. She took a roundabout route instead, walking halfway around the square on the sidewalk to reach the tiny shop that was squeezed in between the milliner's and the hatter's. It was a tiny, narrow building, with a thin door and a single window displaying a few modest gloves arranged hopefully behind the glass. Business was always slow, but so was Dinah's arithmetic, so perhaps that was for the best.

She pushed the door open and heard the familiar little chime of the silver bell that hung over the door. Mr. Beagle, the glover, looked up from where he was hunched over a workbench, painstakingly sewing a leather pad onto a pair of custom-made riding gloves. He was a wizened little old widower with a gleaming, bald head, sporting great tufts of white hair above each ear. They floated in the air like candy floss when he turned his head to smile at her.

"Good morning, Mrs. Hughes," he said.

Dinah forced a smile for him. "Hello, Mr. Beagle."

"I trust you had a good night?" said Mr. Beagle, screwing his monocle a little deeper into his face as he turned back to his work.

"Yes, thank you, sir. I slept well," said Dinah. She sat down on her stool behind the counter, opening a new page in the ledger.

"Yet you still seem so tired today," said Mr. Beagle. "The loss of your husband weighs heavily on you, Mrs. Hughes."

"It does," sighed Dinah. "I try not to think about it too much, yet..." She shook her head. "I find my joy wherever I can, sir, and your kindness is one place that seldom fails."

Mr. Beagle smiled. "Yes, my dear, but you still seem so lonely."

"I am," Dinah admitted. "My brother is doing so well at school, and Geoffrey and Letitia are so good to him..." She looked up at Mr. Beagle. "Sir, if I may speak plainly, sometimes it feels like I've outlived my usefulness."

Mr. Beagle set down the half-finished glove and removed his monocle to give her a stern look. "Now why would a nice young woman like you think something like that?" he asked.

"All I ever lived for was to make sure Ollie had a good future," said Dinah. "Now he no longer needs me. He has everything he needs to have a good, successful life. There was a time that I hoped perhaps Bartholomew and I would have a life together..." She sighed, shaking her head. "I don't know that there's anything left for me in this world." *My greatest dream of all can never come true*, she added in her heart, thinking of Benjamin.

"Well now, Mrs. Hughes," said Mr. Beagle, "you'll forgive me if I dare say to you that your words are the most utter, complete and total codswallop I had ever heard."

His forceful voice startled her. She stared at him. "I beg your pardon?"

"You are talking unadulterated rubbish, Mrs. Hughes," said Mr. Beagle. "Look at you. You're young, and clever, and kind – and you have your whole life ahead of you. Don't you know how many people there are in this world who need people like you, people with good hearts, who can be helpful?"

Dinah stared at him. Abruptly, her heart fled back to the little girl she'd once been, sweating through those fourteen-hour shifts in the match factory in a wild bid to find some way to keep food in Ollie's belly and a roof over his heart. A pulse of guilt ran through her. If only there had been someone like she was now who had reached out a helping hand to the lost little child she was, perhaps her story would have ended very differently.

"You're right, Mr. Beagle," she said, blinking back tears as she looked down at the empty ledger. "You're quite right."

Mr. Beagle got up from his workbench and laid a fatherly hand on her shoulder. "I don't mean to be sharp with you, dear Mrs. Hughes," he said. "But I know the cure for the depression you feel. Mrs. Beagle and I always used to go over to the orphanage near the old church of a Sunday afternoon and read to the children. I tend their gardens for them now, although perhaps not very well, with my old back." He chuckled softly. "But there's no one to read to them. Come with me next Sunday. They would love to have your company. I assume you can read."

Dinah found herself smiling at the thought. It was the first time she had smiled in a long, long time.

"Very well, Mr. Beagle," she said. "My reading isn't the best, but I think that sounds like an excellent idea."

THE SHAMED LITTLE MATCH GIRL

THE DINING HALL of the orphanage echoed with shouts and laughter. Likely it was usually a depressing place, with its tiny windows and hard wooden benches, but now the hall was alive with voices. Dinah could feel her cheeks heating with exertion, but it was pleasant, invigorating, to feel the pounding of her heart. With a child's hand in each of her own, she was nearly too breathless to sing as they skipped in a circle, the little bare feet of the orphans slapping on the unforgiving stone floor.

"Ring-a-ring-a-rosie." she sang. "A pocketful of posies."

The children – all of them less than ten years old – were not so much singing along as shouting at the top of their lungs. Their volume reached an incredible level as they continued the rhyme. "Atishoo. Atishoo. We all fall down."

Dinah laughed as they all fell flat to the ground. The floor was grubby, smearing her modest cotton dress, but she couldn't bring herself to care. It was just too wonderful to be among these laughing children. Their eyes were so bright despite their pinched little faces, and the way they looked at her made her feel like she belonged.

Perhaps she did belong now, she reflected, watching the little boy nearest her writhe on his back as he squealed with laughter. Summer had come gloriously to London, and in the past few months, the children at the orphanage had come to enjoy their Sunday afternoons with Dinah almost as much as she did.

"All right." she said, bouncing to her feet and clapping her hands. "Who's ready for a game of blind man's bluff?"

"No one, I'm afraid," said a stern voice from the door of the dining hall.

Dinah and the children looked up. The orphanage matron, an unsmiling woman with severe gray eyes, was standing in the doorway. "It's time for supper," she said.

"No," squealed the little boy, grabbing Dinah's hand. "I don't want Mrs. Hughes to go."

"Don't worry, Alfred." Dinah bent down to kiss his little forehead. "I'll be back again on Sunday. You be a good boy now."

The little ones trailed around her skirt and legs, giving her a long communal embrace, and Dinah made sure to kiss each one of them on the cheek before they scampered to their places at the bare tables. The matron managed something like a smile when she reached the door. "Thank you for coming," she said. "The children do love you."

"I love them," said Dinah. "They bring meaning to my life." She smiled. "I'll see you next week."

"Next week," nodded the matron.

Dinah tied on her hat and stepped out into a balmy Sunday evening. The weather was splendid; the golden light of the late sun poured over the streets, and if they were a little grimy in this part of town, then they just felt a little more like home to Dinah. She tipped back her head, enjoying the warmth of the sun on her face. It was nice enough, but like the children's laughter, it could never quite heal all the broken places inside her.

Nor could it fill that great void that still seemed to live in the center of her heart. She tried to fill it with spending time with the children, yet it only ever seemed to grow and grow.

"Dinah?"

Dinah stopped and turned around. The first thrill that ran through her was one of perfect joy. How else could it be, when she was looking into a pair of eyes so deeply forest green that they seemed to throb with life, with hope, with purpose? Her whole heart seemed to take wing and lift, but only for a moment before the second thrill of utter shock and pain ran through her.

Benjamin was right there in front of her. But there was a woman on his arm.

For a long, trembling moment, Dinah could only stare at her. She seemed vaguely familiar in some way, and she was smiling, but her hand was resting very securely on Benjamin's elbow, her body very close to his own. She was wearing elegant white gloves, and Dinah couldn't make out if she was wearing a ring or not. But their proximity said it all; he had married and left her behind in his past, just as she had married and left him, and she knew a terrible ache in her soul that felt almost ready to tear her apart from the inside.

"Oh, Dinah, it *is* you." said Benjamin. He took a hurrying step toward her, then hesitated, stopping a few feet short of her. Of course. He was a married man now. There would be no catching her up into his arms anymore. "How... how are you?" he asked haltingly.

Dinah wanted to scream and flee and forget how much she loved him, how passionately her heart was still throbbing for him as their eyes met, but she couldn't. Somehow, she forced a smile. "I'm quite well, thank you," she said. "How are you?"

"I'm well," said Benjamin.

They stared at one another for a few more moments. Benjamin's wife watched them, saying nothing, a faint smile on her lips.

"How is Ollie?" Benjamin asked.

"He's very well." Dinah smiled for real this time. "I'm going to have Sunday dinner with him now. He's going to be a second-year at school in the autumn. His headmaster says he is one of the most promising boys in the entire school."

"Oh, Dinah, that's wonderful," said Benjamin, his eyes shining with real pleasure. "I'm glad to hear it. And how is... ah..." He shifted uncomfortably, clearing his throat. "How is your husband?"

"He's dead," said Dinah, a little more quickly than she meant. "He died last summer."

"Oh." Benjamin hesitated. "I'm sorry to hear that."

"Yes." Dinah lowered her eyes, hoping he couldn't see the guilt and shame that filled them. "How about you? How is your stable?"

"It's doing very well. I have my own cottage right by the stable," said Benjamin, grinning with real pleasure. "I'm saving up to build a stable of my own one day – it'll take a few years, but it's going very well."

Dinah felt a deep, aching joy rise in her. Benjamin was beaming with pride, and he looked so happy with his pretty little wife on his arm and his shoulders broad and strong with prosperity. He was so happy that it was hard not to be happy herself, even though she knew she couldn't share his joy – not the way she would have wanted to.

"I'm very glad for you," she said softly.

Benjamin's eyes were soulful as they met hers. For a long moment, neither of them spoke; they simply gazed. Then Benjamin's wife made a small, throat-clearing sound, and he startled a little. Dinah felt her cheeks heat up in shame at being caught staring at another woman's husband in that way.

"Ah, Dinah," said Benjamin, clearing his throat. He laid a hand over his wife's where it rested on his arm. "I'm sure you remember my sister, Pearl."

Sister? For a moment, Dinah's world felt utterly knocked askew. She blinked at Benjamin, then at the woman, and she recognized her at last. It had been eight years since she'd last laid eyes on Pearl Morris, and an easier life had wiped away the worried lines from her face and the pinched look from her cheeks, but now she recognized her at last. An incredulous laugh tore loose from her throat.

"Pearl," she said. "You look so well, I didn't recognize you at all." She held out her arms, hugging her old friend. "I'm so happy to see you're doing so well."

Pearl held Dinah's hands, and her eyes flickered from Dinah to Benjamin. A slow smile played around her lips. "Benji, dear," she said, turning to her brother, "I'm a little tired for the walk home. Would you mind hailing a cab for me?"

"Of course," said Benjamin. He hesitated. "Would you like to ride in our cab with us, Dinah?" he asked.

"Oh, yes, yes, please," said Dinah quickly, before her thoughts or doubts could get in the way; the words simply leaped out of her.

"Benji, don't be silly." Pearl laughed. "Look at Dinah – she's not tired at all. And the weather is glorious. Why don't you walk her home instead?"

Benjamin met Dinah's eyes. Something flickered in them, something that reached down far below all of Dinah's fears and stirred a part of her that went deeper than guilt or fear. A part of her that seemed to glow and fill every cell in her body, to push aside her misgivings, to push aside everything except the look in Benjamin's eyes.

"Yes," he said softly, holding out his arm. "I think that's a wonderful idea."

Dinah stared at him for a moment, feeling fear tug at her. What would he say if he found out she'd lost her baby? What would he say if he found out that Bartholomew had died because of her? Perhaps she should just walk away and leave Benjamin to the happy life he was building for himself...

But she looked into his eyes. And they still held the memory of that tree in Whitechapel, the only beauty she had known in that hard time, the only symbol of life she had been able to cling to. The memory of them had borne her through so much. The presence of him could bear her through so much more.

She took his arm. "I think it's a wonderful idea, too," she said.

CHAPTER 14

Three Years Later

Tears of exertion, fear, and pain poured down Dinah's face as she lay back in the little bed, propped up on a pile of pillows. Her world was a haze of agony; every muscle trembled, her fingers shaking uncontrollably where she clung to Pearl's hand. For a moment, darkness swarmed around her, and Dinah thought she might faint. But she pushed it aside. She had to listen. She had to hear...

A thin cry rose through the air in the tiny bedroom of the cottage. It was a piercing, wailing, grating sound, yet Dinah had never heard anything so pricelessly beautiful.

"She's all right." Pearl gasped beside her. "Oh, Dinah, she's just fine." She reached over and brushed some of Dinah's hair out of her face, grinning widely. "It's a little girl, and she's beautiful. She's just beautiful."

Joy bloomed in Dinah's heart like a sunrise. "A girl," she panted, sweat trickling down her cheeks. "A little girl." She let go of Pearl's hand and held out her arms. "Give her to me. Oh, please, give her."

"Mama's just cleaning her. Wait just a minute, dear," said Pearl.

Dinah blinked hard to clear her blurry vision and saw Aggie coming toward her, a little bundle swaddled in her arms. She let out a little cry of delight as Aggie grinned at her, her wrinkled face a picture of joy. "My little granddaughter," she said, her voice cracking. "Dinah, she's just beautiful. And she's a healthy, healthy baby."

She bent, lowering the baby to Dinah's chest, and she let out a breath of total awe and joy as she stared down at the little pink creature bundled up in the clean swaddling clothes. Her baby was perfect. She had a few faint wisps of blonde hair, and a little button nose that reminded her of Ollie.

"Hello, darling," Dinah breathed, aware of the tears streaming down her cheeks. She looked up at Aggie. "Please, may I see Benjamin?"

Aggie and Pearl exchanged a glance. "Dinah, you really should have a few hours to rest," said Pearl gently.

"Please," said Dinah.

"I think five minutes will be all right," said Aggie. "He's been pacing the hall all morning, poor soul. Then you must sleep."

Dinah nodded. "And you'll write to Ollie, won't you, Aggie?"

"Straight away." Aggie grinned. "He'll be so glad to hear that he's an uncle. At least, it's nearly summer, and he can meet the little one when he comes back from school."

THE SHAMED LITTLE MATCH GIRL

Aggie and Pearl bustled off, and a few moments later, the door to the little bedroom opened and Benjamin came in. He clutched his cap in his hands and his face was very pale, but the sight of him still made Dinah's heart turn over, just as it had on their wedding day two years ago. When his eyes found her, they widened in nervousness. "Di," he croaked.

"Oh, Benji, my darling." Dinah let out a little laugh. "Come and look at our baby girl." Tears of relief ran down her cheeks. "I did it, Benjamin. I gave you a baby."

Benjamin leaned over her and kissed her forehead. "You were already enough for me," he whispered. "This is... this is more than I ever dreamed of."

He looked down at the baby, and Dinah saw the delight spreading over his face as he gazed at his newborn daughter. She felt her own heart swell almost too big for her chest to contain. In just a few more years, Benjamin would have enough money to build a livery stable. Soon their little girl would be toddling around a property that they owned, playing with Ollie when he came home from the school where he was still excelling, growing up in a life of joy and abundance. Her daughter would never be hungry, never work in a match factory, never marry a man that she didn't love out of sheer desperation.

This child would be happy and free all her life. Dinah knew there would be trials along the way, but she also knew that if she and Benjamin were together, all would be well.

The baby stirred slightly and opened her eyes. They were forest green.

The End

CONTINUE READING...

THANK you for reading ***The Shamed Little Match Girl!* Are you wondering what to read next?** Why not read ***The Little Christmas Waif?* Here's a sneak peek for you:**

Vickey Cooper had often heard the rich folk who came to stay at her mistress' manor house talking about the "Christmas Spirit." They used words like *jolly*, and *festive*, and talked about how everything was *magical*.

Even though it was two weeks before Christmas right now, that magic felt a very long way away. Kneeling by the kitchen grate, Vickey blinked back tears as she polished away, her fingers numb with cold and exhaustion. Her knees ached on the cold stone floor, and there was a draft blowing in under the back door that whistled around her threadbare uniform.

She was eleven hours into a fourteen-hour day, and tiredness was making her hands tremble. Gritting her teeth against the cold that turned them numb, she felt a shiver run through her as she worked at the grate, trying to bring it to some kind of a

THE SHAMED LITTLE MATCH GIRL

shine. It made no sense to her that her mistress, rich dowager Miss Watson, had decreed that every single grate in the entire house needed to be polished by Christmas. It wasn't as if any of the rich guests she entertained – ladies in fine silk and men in neatly cut suits – would ever dream of setting foot in this kitchen or any other. She wondered if any of them even knew what a raw potato looked like.

But Vickey knew, and there was a mound of potatoes waiting for her by the kitchen sink that would have to be peeled and chopped in the next hour for Miss Watson's dinner. It would be a miserable task in the biting cold of the kitchen. Even though she could finally light a fire in this hearth when the polishing was all done, it would take ages to warm the enormous room. She had to hold back tears. There wasn't even a chance of taking some rest on Christmas Day itself – Miss Watson would have a lavish party, and it would be the busiest day of Vickey's whole year.

In fact, Vickey was quite ready to make up her mind that Christmas was the worst time of year when a little giggle danced through the air like sunlight on rippling water. She couldn't help smiling as she sat back on her heels for a minute, looking over her shoulder at the blanket she'd spread out in the corner.

"Now what are you up to, Cara?" she asked softly.

The child on the blanket looked up, striking Vickey as she always did with her nearly angelic beauty. Shining locks of russet-brown hair poured over her shoulders, their grubbiness unable to hide their bounce and radiance. Freckles were scattered like fairy dust over her pert little nose, which turned up at the end as delicately as a flower petal, and she had tremendous dark eyes so large and so limpid that they put Vickey in mind of some deep well of fresh, cool water.

"What are you giggling about, my little hummingbird?" Vickey asked.

Cara beamed at her, her plump cheeks rising adorably against her eyes, chubby with toddlerhood despite the fact that her arms and legs were stick-thin for want of good food. "You so pwetty, Mama," she said, the fat syllables sliding off her clumsy baby tongue.

Click Here to Continue Reading!
http://www.ticahousepublishing.com/victorian-romance.html

THANKS FOR READING

IF YOU LOVE VICTORIAN ROMANCE, Click Here

https://victorian.subscribemenow.com/

to hear about all **New Faye Godwin Romance Releases! I will let you know as soon as they become available!**

Thank you, Friends! If you enjoyed ***The Shamed Little Match Girl,*** would you kindly take a couple minutes to leave a positive review on Amazon? It only takes a moment, and positive reviews truly make a difference. Thank you so much! I appreciate it!

Much love,

Faye Godwin

MORE FAYE GODWIN VICTORIAN ROMANCES!

We love rich, dramatic Victorian Romances and have a library of Faye Godwin titles just for you! (Remember that ALL of Faye's Victorian titles can be downloaded FREE with Kindle Unlimited!)

CLICK HERE to discover Faye's Complete Collection of Victorian Romance!
https://ticahousepublishing.com/victorian-romance.html

ABOUT THE AUTHOR

Faye Godwin has been fascinated with Victorian Romance since she was a teen. After reading every Victorian Romance in her public library, she decided to start writing them herself —which she's been doing ever since. Faye lives with her husband and young son in England. She loves to travel throughout her country, dreaming up new plots for her romances. She's delighted to join the Tica House Publishing family and looks forward to getting to know her readers.

contact@ticahousepublishing.com

Printed in Great Britain
by Amazon